"The war isn't far away for you, is it?" Laura murmured.

"It's a living hell for you still today."

Morgan held her tightly, feeling the fluttering beat of her generous heart. God, he had to get hold of himself. For her sake. He wanted to love her, right now . . . but he wouldn't drag her into his morbid, complicated life.

"Listen to me," he said harshly. "Don't open yourself up to me and my problems."

Laura took a deep, unsteady breath. "It's my nature to get involved, Morgan."

"Then fight for someone worth fighting for."

Forcing a slight smile, she said, "I guess I'm letting this trauma get to me."

"Yeah, a close call with death can make you do things you're sorry for later," Morgan agreed.

Backing away from her, he saw the stubborn set of her chin and the spark of defiance in her eyes. And those warming seconds he'd spent in her arms made him starved to explore her. All of her . . .

Dear Reader,

This month Silhouette **Special Edition** brings you the third (though not necessarily the last) volume of Lindsay McKenna's powerful **LOVE AND GLORY** miniseries, and we'd love to know if the *Return of a Hero* moves you as much as it did our Silhouette editors. Many of you write in requesting sequels or tie-in books—now we'd like to hear how you enjoyed our response!

Many of you also urge us to publish more books by your favorite Silhouette authors, and with this month's lively selection of novels by Jo Ann Algermissen, Carole Halston, Bevlyn Marshall, Natalie Bishop and Maggi Charles, we hope we've satisfied that craving, as well.

Each and every month our Silhouette **Special Edition** authors and editors strive to bring you the ultimate in satisfying romance reading. Although we cannot answer your every letter, we do take your comments and requests to heart. So, many thanks for your help—we hope you'll keep coming back to Silhouette **Special Edition** to savor the results!

From all the authors and editors of Silhouette **Special Edition**,

Warmest wishes,

Leslie Kazanjian, Senior Editor
Silhouette Books
300 East 42nd Street
New York, N.Y. 10017

LINDSAY McKENNA
Return of a Hero

Silhouette Special Edition

Published by Silhouette Books New York

America's Publisher of Contemporary Romance

SILHOUETTE BOOKS
300 East 42nd St., New York, N.Y. 10017

ISBN: 0-373-09541-4

First Silhouette Books printing August 1989

All the characters in this book are fictitious. Any
resemblance to actual persons, living or dead, is
purely coincidental.

®: Trademark used under license and
registered in the United States Patent and
Trademark Office and in other countries.

Printed in the U.S.A.

Books by Lindsay McKenna

Silhouette Special Edition

Captive of Fate #82
*Heart of the Eagle #338
*A Measure of Love #377
*Solitaire #397
Heart of the Tiger #434
†A Question of Honor #529
†No Surrender #535
†Return of a Hero #541

Silhouette Intimate Moments

Love Me Before Dawn #44

Silhouette Desire

Chase the Clouds #75
Wilderness Passion #134
Too Near the Fire #165
Texas Wildcat #184
Red Tail #298

*Kincaid trilogy
†LOVE AND GLORY series

Awards:

1984 Journalism Award for fiction books from the Aviation/Space Writers Association for *Love Me Before Dawn*, Silhouette Intimate Moments #44

1985 Journalism Award for fiction books from the Aviation/Space Writers Association for *Red Tail*, Silhouette Desire #298

1987 *Romantic Times* Best Continuing Series Author Award for the Kincaid trilogy, Silhouette Special Edition (#338, #377, #397)

Waldenbooks Romance Bestseller:

1985 *Texas Wildcat*, Silhouette Desire

LINDSAY McKENNA

spent three years serving her country as a meteorologist in the U.S. Navy, so much of her knowledge about the military people and practices featured in her novels comes from direct experience. In addition, she spends a great deal of time researching each book, whether it be at the Pentagon or at military bases, extensively interviewing key personnel. She views the military as her second family and hopes that her novels will help dispel the "unfeeling-machine" image that haunts it, allowing readers glimpses of the flesh-and-blood people who comprise the services.

Lindsay is also a pilot. She and her husband of fifteen years, both avid "rock hounds" and hikers, live in Ohio.

LOVE AND GLORY: BOOK III

The Trayherns

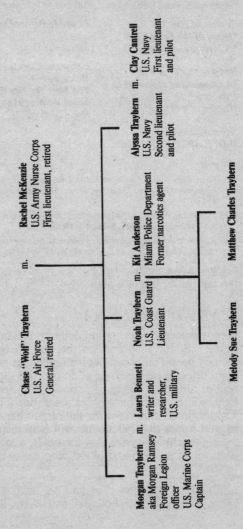

Chase "Wolf" Trayhern
U.S. Air Force
General, retired

m.

Rachel McKenzie
U.S. Army Nurse Corps
First lieutenant, retired

Morgan Trayhern
aka Morgan Ramsey
Foreign Legion
officer
U.S. Marine Corps
Captain

m.

Laura Bennett
writer and
researcher,
U.S. military

Noah Trayhern
U.S. Coast Guard
Lieutenant

m.

Kit Anderson
Miami Police Department
Former narcotics agent

Alyssa Trayhern
U.S. Navy
Second lieutenant
and pilot

m.

Clay Cantrell
U.S. Navy
First lieutenant
and pilot

Melody Sue Trayhern

Matthew Charles Trayhern

Chapter One

It was raining. *Or is the sky crying?* Morgan Trayhern wondered as he climbed out of the black limousine. The dawn sky above Washington, D.C., was a funereal gray, mirroring his feelings. Water ran down the planes of his tense face as he walked up a red brick path toward an old Georgian manor tucked away behind a number of sycamore and elm trees.

Fatigue lapped at Morgan as he hunched more deeply into his trench coat. Yesterday he'd received a directive from the commandant of the French Foreign Legion to report to headquarters. Orders had come from American officials, asking him to return at once to Washington for an unspecified reason. The commandant assured him that although the marine corps officials had urgently requested his presence, once the meeting was over, he could return to France and resume his duties as an officer in the Legion. Further, this unexpected trip was top secret. His commanding officer couldn't even name the man who had issued the orders that had brought him stateside after a seven-year absence. The whole situation made Morgan apprehensive, and a nine-hour flight from France, coupled with time changes, had stripped him, leaving him raw and uneasy.

Morgan saw that the door to the manor was open. A marine corps general in a dark-green uniform filled the entranceway, peering out at him through the pall. Wrestling with his surprise and the sudden pounding of his heart, Morgan clenched one of his fists. So, General Kip Young, his commanding officer back in 1970, wanted to see him. The bastard.

As Morgan approached the door, the bulldog-jawed general with thinning gray hair beckoned him to enter. "Captain Morgan Trayhern?"

Flooded with unexpected anger, Morgan nodded. "You know it is." Maybe his black mustache had changed his appearance more than he'd realized.

Shutting the door, the general stepped back, allowing the maid to take Morgan's trench coat. "General Jack Armstrong is dying. As you know, he was in charge of your battalion."

Glaring at Young, Morgan straightened his dark pin-striped jacket. "Is he dying of guilt, sir?"

"Now you look here," Young snarled, coming within inches of him. "You keep a civil tongue in your head. Jack Armstrong saved your life seven years ago.''

A thin, cutting smile slashed across Morgan's mouth. "And I'm supposed to be grateful for his turning me into a convenient scapegoat and purported traitor to my country so that he and all his cronies could escape the blame for Hill 164?'' Morgan defiantly held Young's steely stare.

"Even though you're in the French Foreign Legion, I expect military courtesy from you, Captain.'' Young's square face turned scarlet. "I'm the one who sent the request to have you fly here. Jack Armstrong is my best friend, and he's dying. There are some things he wants to get off his chest and they involve you.''

Taking a quick look around the impressive home whose walls were filled with war mementos from Armstrong's thirty-year military career, Morgan shrugged. "I'm following orders from Commandant Gérard. I didn't want to come, General. If I'd realized you were behind this visit—or that Armstrong wanted to talk to me—I'd have refused. As soon as this charade's over, I'm catching a plane back to France.'' His voice grew deep. "And you can keep your filthy little secret.''

"Excuse me,'' a maid called to the general. "The doctor says you must hurry.''

Young made a chopping motion toward the walnut-paneled hallway. "Fourth door on the left. Jack is lucid, but Dr. Bonner says he won't last until sundown today. Whatever your personal feelings over this, Captain, I hope you can respect the fact that he's dying.''

Girding himself, swallowing his anger as he'd been doing for the past year, ever since he'd regained his memory of how he'd been used by Armstrong, Morgan gave a brusque nod to indicate that he understood. He followed the worried-looking maid, quickening his stride. The house was dark and shadowy. Young trailed at a safe distance as they moved down the carpeted hallway.

The maid opened the door to the master bedroom, and Morgan stood uncertainly at the entrance. His heart wouldn't stop pounding; so many old emotions were erupting from within him. His gaze took in the room, from the cheerless brown drapes to the massive carved oak bed, where a frail, emaciated Armstrong lay. Everything was morbidly dark in this house. As Morgan stepped inside, Young edged past him and crossed to the bed. Morgan felt his stomach knot with despair.

Dr. Bonner, a robust man of middle age, slipped back into the shadows, his face grim. Young placed his hand on the shoulder of his dying friend.

"Jack?"

The man in the bed stirred briefly. "Kip?"

"It's me."

"You brought him?"

Young looked over at Morgan and motioned him forward. "Yes, he's here. He's standing at the foot of your bed."

His palms suddenly sweaty, Morgan had the wild urge to wipe them on the pin-striped slacks he wore. Instead he stood stiffly, watching the man in the bed. Jack Armstrong's was the first face Morgan had seen when he'd regained consciousness in a hospital in Japan after the slaughter on Hill 164. The same razor-thin face that he had come to hate was now pinched with illness, the cheeks sunken and the skin stretched like parchment across them. Morgan took a deep breath, wanting to run as Armstrong's lashes fluttered and finally lifted. Those once-piercing green eyes were dull as they settled on him. Morgan felt a scream starting to unwind in his gut, just as it had a year ago when he'd finally realized the truth of who he was and what Armstrong had done to him.

"You . . . came," Armstrong rasped. One corner of his mouth lifted upward briefly.

"Did I have a choice?" Morgan's voice rolled through the hushed room. He saw Young shoot him a warning look that spoke volumes. To hell with all of them. He wasn't going to be kind or courteous after what they'd done to him.

"C-come closer, Morgan. I-I need to tell you—" The old man took several shallow breaths.

Reluctantly Morgan moved to stand next to the general's bed. "Say it, Armstrong."

"I deserve your anger, Morgan," he whispered. "I wanted you to know the full truth. I didn't want to die with this on my conscience. . . ."

Clenching his teeth, Morgan tasted the hate that had eaten at him for a year. "You lied to me, Armstrong. You and whoever else was in on this scheme."

Weakly lifting a hand, Armstrong silenced him. "The CIA persuaded us to send a company of men into an active NVA area. They said it was safe." He took a breath, then closed his eyes for several moments before going on. "My staff and I backed the CIA appraisal of the situation. It was a chance to make a major coup."

"You thought putting my company on Hill 164 would earn you another star," Morgan hissed. "And it did, didn't it?"

"Y-yes. One that I've worn with guilt ever since." Armstrong opened his eyes and stared fiercely up at Morgan. "I had removed all air support to another part of Vietnam, thinking your company would be safe. I left you defenseless—but not on purpose. It was a horrible tactical error. By the time our helicopter got there, only two of you were left alive. You and Private Lenny Miles."

"And you chose me as your scapegoat, didn't you, Armstrong?" Though anger thrummed through Morgan, this specter on the bed before him brought out only a pathetic numbness.

"We had no choice," Armstrong cried softly, tears welling in his eyes. "My entire staff would have been sent home in disgrace. There would have been court martials. I couldn't see the lives of five good officers destroyed like that." Wheezing, he sank back into the pillows, gathering strength. "A plan was brought to my attention after we found you alive. You had received massive wounds to the head and chest. By the time we got you to Japan for treatment, the doctors told us you'd sustained brain damage, as well. They didn't think you'd survive. So we sent word to the press and our superiors that you had deserted your post, leaving your company of men open to NVA attack. I thought it would be only a matter of hours before you died. That's why I let you be the scapegoat."

"And what about Lenny Miles?" Morgan ground out.

"He was only slightly wounded, but he'd been on drugs, so we had him. We threatened him with court martial if he didn't go along with our plan. Miles didn't want to end up at a military prison, busting rocks for the next thirty years."

"So he agreed."

"He had no choice."

"And when I managed to survive my wounds, that threw a chink into your plans, didn't it, Armstrong?"

The general sighed. "Yes. On the suggestion of someone in the CIA, I flew to your bedside. The doctors told me you had amnesia and couldn't recall anything about your family or past—not even your name. So, as you remember, I sat there telling you how you'd been wounded as a CIA operative behind the lines in Laos. You had no recall of 164 or losing your company of men, so you swallowed the story line."

A harsh smile shadowed Morgan's mouth. "I can still remember you at my bedside, filling me in on every detail, Armstrong. You gave me a new name—

Morgan Ramsey. And you told me I had no family, that I was an orphan." His voice trembled. "You gave me an entirely different life. For six years I didn't really know who I was or what had happened to my company. I believed everything you told me, because I couldn't remember a thing. I didn't see a newspaper in Japan for the first three months because I was lapsing in and out of a mild coma state. By the time I could read or watch television, the furor over my 'desertion' and role in the destruction of my company was over."

"After nine months in the hospital, you'd recovered sufficiently to be sent to the French Foreign Legion."

"Where I thought I was being patriotic by becoming a CIA mole within that organization."

"Yes." Armstrong's eyes watered. "And until a year ago, you didn't really know who or what you were."

"I lived in hell for that year," Morgan said, an edge to his voice, "thanks to you."

"I—I just wanted to say I'm sorry it had to be someone like you. Sometimes one good man has to be sacrificed for the good of all...." He closed his eyes.

Morgan stood, a violent storm of emotions flooding him. He watched the doctor move to the bed and pick up Armstrong's wrist to take his pulse. Bonner looked over at him.

"I think you'd better leave, Captain Ramsey. He won't be with us much longer. His pulse is failing."

A powerful urge to scream settled over Morgan. He turned on his heel and jerked open the door, his breath coming in sharp rasps as he moved down the dreary hall toward the foyer. All he wanted to do was escape.

"Captain!" Young caught up with him in the foyer and gripped him by the arm.

Morgan wheeled around, wrenching out of the officer's grasp. "Stay the hell away from me," he breathed savagely. His trench coat hung in the closet, and he yanked it off the hanger.

Young's face broadcast wariness. "What are you going to do now that you know what really happened?"

Shrugging into the trench coat, Morgan glared at Young. "Not a damn thing, General. I know that if I tried to clear my name, you'd make sure I was stopped at every turn."

"You're right. I think it's best if you catch the next flight back to France. At least there you have a good life."

The urge to punch the arrogant general in his flushed face was strong. "Good life!" he spit. "I have parents who grieve for me. I have a brother and sister I haven't seen for years. You've not only hurt me— you've hurt them, as well." Punching a finger into Young's chest, Morgan whispered harshly, "If I didn't have to involve them in clearing my name, I'd do it in an instant, Young. But I know the Pentagon and I know the military machine. You'd use the press to your advantage and put such ungodly pressure on my family that it wouldn't be worth it." His breathing was ragged as he straightened and tied the belt around his waist. "Don't look so worried, Young. I'll keep my cover. I've got reenlistment papers for another five-year stint waiting for me back in Marseilles. They want to make me a major if I sign over." His nostrils flared. "I can live out my life in a dingy third world country, fighting wars I couldn't care less about."

Young backed off. "The limo will take you out to the airport," he said stiffly. "Thank you for coming."

"You're a pack of bastards," Morgan snarled, opening the door. Outside, he felt the rain slash at his face as he walked down the brick path. The water cooled the hot frustration inside him. He lifted his face and deeply inhaled the wet springtime air.

Inside the limo, he snapped at the chauffeur, "Get me the hell out of here and back to the airport."

Sinking into the gloom of the back seat, Morgan closed his eyes. Tears welled beneath his lids, and he swallowed against his constricted throat. The sky was crying. He was on U.S. soil for the first time in seven years and Clearwater, Florida, where his parents lived, was only an hour-and-a-half flight from D.C.

He dragged in a shaky breath, then opened his eyes and glared out into the gray light. The beauty of Georgetown escaped him as he focused on the pain in his heart. How was Noah? One week before Morgan's company had been wiped out, Noah's Coast Guard career had been in high gear. And Aly... Tears squeezed from beneath his short, spiky lashes. Groaning, he covered his face with his large, scarred hand. Had her dreams of getting an appointment to Annapolis been fulfilled? Had she graduated to go on to Pensacola? All she'd ever wanted was to fly.

It hurt to think of them like this. In France his life revolved around his men, a barracks and soldiering duty on Corsica, where the Legion had one of its forts. The men who were in the Legion came from around the world. Most of them had changed their names, never discussing their pasts with anyone.

Wiping his eyes, Morgan fought to get a hold on himself. The last time he'd cried was when his memory had returned. Over the years, he'd had dreams, seen faces, but had never been able to put them together. Then, on a cliff-climbing exercise in France, his rope had snapped and he'd plummeted thirty feet to the ground. When he'd regained consciousness, the memory of who and what he really was had started to come back.

The limo eased to a halt at a concrete island in front of Pan Am Airlines. The rain was worsening. Morgan muttered his thanks to the driver and got out. All he had was a small leather satchel containing one set of clean clothes. Cars were whizzing by, coming and going like frantic bees to a hive.

The rain was soothing, and Morgan stood on the concrete island, lifting his face to the cleansing power of it. The tormented desire to stay and see his family warred with reality. He couldn't just walk back into their lives unannounced. If the press found out he was back, they'd have a field day. The mustache helped change the look of his face. So did the long scar that ran from his temple down his cheek and followed the square line of his jaw. No, it was unlikely that even his family would recognize the proud young marine captain of 1970 who'd posed with his company of men weeks before the tragedy.

Morgan opened his eyes, tasting the salt of his tears in the corners of his mouth. It was eight in the morning. The sidewalk was jammed with people, and hordes of businessmen were streaming into the busy airport facility. They were all dressed in dark trench coats and carried umbrellas and expensive briefcases. Suddenly the color pink caught his attention.

Directly across the four lanes of traffic, standing on the curb and trying to cross, was a woman in her late twenties. Morgan seized upon her; she was like a bright flower among the grays, browns and blacks of the business suits and coats. Small and slender, she reminded Morgan of a swan. Maybe she was one, he decided, trying to put his suffering behind him. There was a serenity to her oval face. Was it her large blue eyes? Or her delicate mouth that curved naturally upward at the corners? Her blond shoulder-length hair was dampened by the rain as she stood impatiently on first one heel, then the other, trying to time her crossing to where he stood.

Beautiful wasn't the word Morgan would have used to describe her. *Intriguing*, yes. The pink raincoat emphasized her slimness. Her eyes were a deep blue, and they sparkled with life. Morgan yearned to feel what the woman exuded. She was like a springtime flower—alive, young and filled with hope. He glanced up at the gray, turbulent sky, and realized he'd been staring at her. But just looking at her calmed him.

Laura watched the swiftly moving traffic with mounting frustration. Each time she tried to cross, another van or limo raced by, sending up sheets of rain in its wake. Something really ought to be done about this, she fumed. Checking the gold watch on her left wrist, she saw that time was running short. If she wanted to make that interview with General Cunningham over at McLean, Virginia, she was going to have to hurry!

Agitated with the arrogant Washington drivers, who never seemed to respect pedestrians, she looked across to the concrete island where she'd be able to catch a taxi. Her attention focused on one man standing among the others. His face was lifted to the rain, as if he were enjoying the sensation of water trickling down it. He was tall and powerful looking, even in the trench coat. Laura was drawn to his face: square, with harsh lines around his mouth and crinkles at the corner of each eye. He was darkly tanned, telling her that he wasn't from this area. April in D.C. was cloudy and dreary with rain. Sunshine was at a premium. The black mustache emphasized the breadth of the man's features. His gray eyes were sharp and intelligent.

The word *mercenary* sprang to Laura's mind, and she chastised her overactive imagination. But there was nothing peaceful about the man's face or his stance. Even from this distance, she could feel the tension in him. Despite his demeanor, Laura's heart went out to him the instant his eyes met and held hers.

There was incredible sadness and turmoil in them. He looked as if he'd just lost his best friend. The rain made his face glisten, but she could almost swear he was crying. Could that be? A scar ran the length of the right side of his face, giving his expression an impenetrable quality.

A gasp broke from Laura. She watched in sudden horror as the man stepped off the curb—and right into the oncoming traffic. Didn't he see that gray limo?

Laura leaped from the safety of the curb, her hand raised in warning. "Look out!" she cried. Desperately she caught his attention, but he seemed dazed, perplexed by her warning. The limo bore down on him. It would be only seconds before he was struck. With a foolhardy lunge, she threw herself at him. Her hands connected solidly with his left shoulder, spinning him around and backward.

She heard the screech of tires on the pavement. Just as the man was thrown off his feet and out of the range of the limo, she felt the impact. One second she was on her feet; the next, she was flying through the air.

Morgan landed heavily against the curb as the limo screamed to a halt beside him. The smell of burned rubber filled the air. Wet and confused, he stumbled to his feet. The woman in the pink raincoat was sprawled ten feet in front of the limo. She had saved his life. The limo driver leaped from the vehicle, his face filled with terror. Cries and shrieks erupted around Morgan, but he ignored them as he ran to the woman's side. Struggling out of his trench coat, he threw it across her to protect her from the downpour. He knelt, his hand going immediately to her small shoulder. She was unconscious, a large, bloody cut on the side of her head, near her left eye. She looked like a bird with a broken wing, so fragile and vulnerable. Dammit!

He looked up at a policeman who had worked his way through the gathering crowd. "Get an ambulance!" Morgan snarled. "Now!" More people ran over. Morgan's hand on her shoulder tightened. My God, she looked dead, her skin waxen. Was she? Shakily he slid his wet fingers around her wrist. There was a pulse—a weak one. Numbed by the events, he stared down at her wrist. The bones of her hand were tiny in comparison to his. Her flesh was so white and smooth; his sun-darkened, with years of calluses built up on the palms.

The vigilant throng pressed closer. Morgan glared up at them. "Give her room to breathe!" he ordered and they enlarged the circle. He leaned over, gently cupping her cheek with his palm. "Hang on," he begged her. "Just hang on, lady. Help's coming...." He dared not move her. She might have broken bones. She could be paralyzed. And all because of his utter stupidity. God, why hadn't he looked for oncoming traffic before he'd stepped off that curb?

By the time the ambulance arrived, some ten minutes later, Morgan was ready to explode at the cold-blooded curiosity of the people milling around. He hated passersby who gawked. Protecting the woman from the rain, he picked up her purse, tucking it beneath his arm. Anguish filled him as he stared down at her delicate features, now colorless. Why had she done such a foolish thing to save his worthless neck? Yet Morgan knew he'd have done the same thing.

Funny little swan, your courage isn't any match for that tiny body you live within. Her blond lashes lay against her high cheekbones; her lips were parted and slack. The paramedics raced over, bags in hand, carrying an oak body board with them. Morgan moved from his crouched position to stand to one side.

"You know her?" the chief paramedic asked, quickly examining her.

"No, but that doesn't matter. I'm coming with you. She saved me from getting hit by this limo."

The paramedic nodded. "Fine by me. Frank, let's get her on the body board. She might have sustained a back injury."

Numbly Morgan watched them transfer the woman to a thin oak board, then strap her snugly to it. Next came the blankets that would keep her warm. The policeman who'd been directing traffic around the accident came up to him.

"We'll follow you to the hospital, mister. I need to make out a report on this."

"Fine," Morgan agreed tautly, walking toward the rear of the ambulance, where the doors had been thrown open. His mind spun with possibilities. He glanced around. So far no reporters were on the scene. If he was lucky, he'd escape the glare of the cameras. Although his face was altered, he couldn't stand the thought that his family might recognize him, beginning their pain all over again.

Ducking into the ambulance, Morgan sat on the seat opposite the gurney where the woman lay, unconscious. Frank stayed in back with her while his partner drove. He worked quickly, taking a blood pressure reading.

"You got her purse?" he demanded.

Morgan produced it. "Yeah."

"Look for ID. We're gonna need some information for Admissions when we get her to the hospital."

The purse was small and neat, just as she was. Morgan felt shaky inside, adrenaline making him tremble. He opened the wallet and looked at the driver's license. Laura Bennett. Pretty name. Like her. . . . He searched the rest of the wallet for the name of a person to contact about the accident.

A frown formed on his damp brow. "Her name is Laura Bennett," he muttered, glancing over at her. "Is she going to live?"

"Her pulse and respiration are slow. She's in shock. Looks like a major head injury. Rest of her doesn't show any broken bones. But she could have internal injuries—I just don't know."

Flinching, Morgan gripped the wallet. Head injury. That had been the cause of his amnesia. Desperation filled him, and he kept his eyes on Laura. How could someone so small and exquisite have such a brave heart? He reached out and pressed his hand to her shoulder.

"Fight back, Laura," he told her. "Don't give in. I'll be here to help you."

Thankfully, the ride to the hospital was a short one. The ambulance rolled up to the Emergency entrance. *Hurry!* Morgan thought, staying out of the way when the attendants flung open the doors. Grimly he climbed out, following the paramedics through the sliding glass doors. In his hand was Laura Bennett's purse, her identity. And right on his heels were the police officers.

Chapter Two

Chaos reigned as the gurney bearing Laura Bennett was wheeled into the hospital. Morgan stared helplessly at the swinging emergency room doors. He had been pushed aside by a nurse, doctors and paramedics, who had disappeared with Laura's gurney behind the sign that said No Admittance.

"Can we get your statement, mister?" the redheaded police sergeant asked him.

Distracted, Morgan turned to the waiting officers. He held up the purse. "Yeah . . . just a minute. Let me give this to the admitting nurse."

His mind swung between concern for Laura's condition and awareness of the watchful officers as he dropped the purse off at the desk. Pushing several strands of damp hair off his brow, he dug into the breast pocket of his business suit and produced his passport for the police.

The sergeant took it and opened it. "Morgan Ramsey, U.S. citizen. You live in France?"

Putting a tight clamp on his emotions, Morgan kept his voice low and devoid of feeling. "That's right."

"French Foreign Legion?" The cop appraised him for a long time, a look of awe on his meaty face.

"I came on military business. I was about to take a plane back to France when this happened." He didn't intend to add anything to pique the cop's curiosity. The Legion had a mystique to it, and Morgan credited the officer's interest to that. Glancing out the doors to the parking lot, Morgan wondered if the press had been notified. He didn't dare allow his photo to be taken.

"Can you tell us what happened?"

"I stepped off the center island at the airport without looking," Morgan explained. "I should have been more careful, but I was thinking about something else at the time. The woman came from the opposite direction and pushed me out of the way of an oncoming limo, and then she got hit."

"Do you know this woman?"

"No."

"She's sure got guts," the other cop muttered, a note of admiration in his voice as he continued to scribble down notes for his report.

The nurse from Admittance came over. "Sergeant Amato, we've searched Ms. Bennett's belongings, and there's nothing to indicate whom we should notify about her injury.'' She held up an insurance card. ''We called her insurance agent and he said she's got no family.''

''No family?'' Morgan asked, his eyebrows lifting.

''Probably an orphan. Or adopted,'' Amato volunteered, rummaging through the contents of Laura's wallet.

Morgan felt as if a hand were squeezing his heart, and he rubbed his chest distractedly. ''Are you sure?'' He turned to the nurse. ''Where does she live?''

''In McLean, Virginia. We've already called her residence, but there's only an answering machine to take messages.''

Scowling, Morgan said, ''Then I'll be her family until someone can be located.''

The sergeant smiled. ''She saved your neck. That's a nice gesture, Mr. Ramsey. What about that plane back to France you were going to catch?''

''It'll wait until I know she's in capable hands.'' He was responsible for what happened, and he wasn't going to leave her in the lurch.

''Once Ms. Bennett becomes conscious, she'll be able to tell us more,'' the nurse said hopefully. ''I'm sorry, Mr. Ramsey, but you can't just assume responsibility for her unless she gives us permission.''

Rules. They were made to be broken sometimes, Morgan thought darkly, and this was one of those times. But he held his counsel. ''I understand. Just let me know as soon as you can what her condition is.''

The nurse nodded briskly. ''Of course.''

The sergeant finished his report by taking down what little information there was regarding Laura Bennett. He glanced at Morgan. "Thanks for your help, Mr. Ramsey. We might need to talk with you again, so please leave an address and phone number where we can reach you at the nurses' station."

Morgan nodded. "I'm not going anywhere until I hear about Ms. Bennett. After that I'll find a local hotel."

"Good enough. Thanks."

Morgan watched the officers leave. The nurse directed him to a waiting room, and, choosing a brown plastic lounge chair, he sat. Resting his elbows on his long thighs, he clasped his hands, staring down at the black-and-white tiles, his mind whirling with questions, his emotions in utter tumult. He'd memorized Laura's face, from her haunting blue eyes to that delicious mouth of hers. Who was she? And why had he been mesmerized by her? Rubbing his face tiredly, he leaned back and rested his head against the wall, utterly drained. For a long time he'd forgotten there was a God, but now he prayed for the life of Laura Bennett.

Intermittent pain stabbed through Laura's head. Groggily she fought to awaken from the darkness that enveloped her. She heard lowered women's voices somewhere in the distance. As she dragged her hand upward, her fingertips came in contact with the bandages around her eyes. What was going on? Struggling to remember, she focused her attention on the dressing.

"Ms. Bennett?" a woman called.

Laura felt the woman's hand come to rest on her shoulder, and she answered, "Y-yes."

"I'm Nurse Karen Mylnar. You're at Washington Memorial Hospital. Four hours ago you were struck by a car at the airport. Do you remember?"

Licking her dry lips, Laura frowned. She sensed people around her. "Hospital?"

"Yes. You're in a private room. Dr. Taggert is here to speak with you. He's the physician on your case."

John Taggert leaned over her and squeezed her hand. "Laura, I'm Dr. Taggert. Do you have someone we can notify about your injury?"

She took in a deep breath. "No."

"Are you an orphan?"

"I'm adopted, but both my parents are dead."

"I see. Do you remember rushing out in front of a car to save a man from getting hit?"

Laura licked her dry lower lip, the man's grief-stricken face wavering in her memory. How could she ever forget those haunted gray eyes? "Y-yes, I remember..."

"Well, he's safe, but you got hit, instead. You were brought here for treatment. You've got some nasty bruises on your left shoulder and hip, but no internal injuries."

The memory of the man with the black mustache walking out in front of the limo flashed across her mind once again. She remembered his eyes, and how she thought he'd been crying. The rest of the doctor's words were lost as she relived the accident.

"Did you hear me, Ms. Bennett?"

"No...I-I'm sorry," Laura whispered, her head aching fiercely.

"You've sustained a deep cut to your right temple, very close to your eye." Taggert frowned. "Right now, neither of your eyes is responding to light."

"I don't understand." She felt infinitely exhausted.

"It's probably temporary. Tissue swelling could account for the lack of response. We're going to have to wait a couple days for the edema in that area to recede to be sure."

"Sure? Of what?" Suddenly the urge to have that mercenary at her side nearly overwhelmed her. Laura had learned to live alone. She had learned to overcome obstacles without the help of others. His sad gray eyes loomed in her memory.

"You're blind right now, Ms. Bennett. But if I'm correct, it's probably temporary. The blow you took to your head caused it."

Blind? A gasp tore from her, and her hand flew to her bandaged eyes. "No!"

"Easy," Taggert said, capturing her hand and pulling it away from the gauze dressing. "Don't panic yet, Ms. Bennett. In forty-eight hours I'll have a better idea whether your condition is temporary or not."

Panic flooded. "But—I can't be blind!" Her voice cracked.

Patting her hand absently, Taggert said, "Give her a sedative, nurse. Please calm down, Ms. Bennett."

Hot, stinging tears flooded her eyes. Darkness surrounded her. Laura sobbed, fighting to sit up. Her entire body ached. "I don't want a sedative!"

"Take it easy," the doctor murmured. "Listen, the man you saved is outside, waiting to talk to you. His name is Morgan Ramsey, and he won't leave without seeing you."

Morgan Ramsey. Laura leaned back against the pillows, running his name again and again through her mind. "He's here?" Suddenly she needed him. The look in his eyes, despite the harsh cast of his face, told her he was a man of honor, someone she could trust.

"Yes. Maybe talking with him will make you feel better."

"Please, send him in," Laura said, her voice quavering. She wrapped her arms around her gowned body, suddenly very cold and very afraid. Her career depended on her eyes. She couldn't be blind. She just couldn't!

Slipping into the room at Taggert's request, Morgan stood in the ebbing silence after the medical team left. Laura's eyes were bandaged, and he could see that her right cheek was puffy and scratched. She had her arms wrapped against herself, and he sensed her terror.

"Laura, my name is Morgan Ramsey," he said quietly, walking over to her bedside. He allowed his hand to rest on her slumped shoulder. "I'm the guy whose neck you saved."

"Morgan..." His touch was firm, steadying, and his voice was deep, calming her panic. Gradually Laura allowed her arms to relax, and she dropped her hands into her lap. "They said you weren't hurt," she said softly.

Her voice was a sandpapery whisper. Morgan took a pitcher and poured water into a glass, placing it in her hand. "I'm fine. You're the one I'm worried about. Drink this. Maybe you'll feel better."

The water was cooling and bathed her dry throat. Grateful for his sensitivity, Laura handed the glass back to him. "Thank you."

Morgan realized she was trembling as he took the glass from her and set it back on the table. Capturing her hand, he said, "Look, this is awkward as hell, but I owe you my life. I stepped off that curb in another world. If you hadn't pushed me out of the way of that limo, I'd probably be dead by now."

The flesh of his hand was tough, but his grasp was warm and comforting. Laura clung to his hand, needing the stability he automatically provided. "I didn't think. I just reacted," she offered lamely.

He sat down carefully on the edge of the bed, facing her. "Do you always do things out of instinct?" he teased, trying to get her to relax.

Managing a shaky laugh, Laura murmured, "Usually."

"Well, there aren't too many people in this world who would have put their life on the line for the likes of me." He squeezed her cold, damp fingers. "Dr. Taggert told me you can't see. He feels it's temporary, but won't be sure for a couple of days. What can I do for you while you're recovering?''

His voice was incredibly soothing. Laura fought the urge to lean forward and rest against him. ''You were at the airport. Surely you have a flight to catch. Not to mention a family and job to go home to. You can't stay here with me.''

Morgan felt a slight smile soften his features. ''I have no wife or children, Laura. And as for my job, it's overseas and can wait.'' He had thirty days' leave coming to him and he would wire the commandant of the Legion, requesting it. ''They said you have no family,'' he added. ''Maybe I can fill in for a while. Or do you have a friend who can stay with you?''

Laura hung her head, trying to think. Ann Roher, her best friend, was in Europe on assignment for a magazine. Other than that, she had many acquaintances, but no real friends. ''My friend Ann is overseas for the next month. I could hire someone—''

''I won't hear of it.'' Morgan watched her beautifully shaped mouth compress with pain. ''Look,'' he said, reluctantly releasing her hand and standing, ''you get some rest. I'll take care of everything.''

''But—''

''I know I'm a stranger to you, but you can trust me—'' his voice grew hoarse ''—with your life.''

A shiver shot through Laura as she heard the distinct catch in his tone. ''I believe you, Morgan, but I just can't ask you or anyone to—''

''I learned a long time ago that when you're wounded, you should always lean on a buddy for help.

It's an old military custom. You're in one hell of a predicament because of me, Laura, and I won't desert you.''

Overwhelmed by the incredible twist of events, Laura sank back into the pillows. His voice was fierce with barely veiled emotion, as if she'd struck a raw nerve in him.

Morgan took her silence to mean no. "Look, I'll get a room at a hotel near your house. I don't intend to make a burden of myself. You're going to need someone to get groceries and cook for you. And I can drive you where you need to go. Taggert seems to feel you'll have your eyesight back very soon. A little of my time is small payment for what you did for me today."

"All right, I surrender," Laura said with a sigh.

"There are keys in your purse. Are they to your car?"

"Yes. It's a red Toyota MR2 sports car. I have it parked at the airport. The validation ticket is in my wallet."

"I'll get your car, then. How about at home? Any pets to feed?"

Some of Laura's panic was being assuaged by Morgan Ramsey's sensible practicality. His reference to being wounded triggered her curiosity, but there would be time later to find out more about this mysterious stranger who had crashed into her life. "Yes, I've got a baby robin at home. She fell out of the apple tree in my backyard a week ago and broke her leg."

Morgan frowned. "A robin?" Anguish surged through him, and with it, old, poignant memories of another baby robin that had touched his life. Was there no end to the pain this day was creating for him? The only positive was Laura. She looked incredibly frail in the stark hospital bed.

"Oh, dear... Will you know how to feed the little bird? She needs worms and fruit—"

"I know all about robins," Morgan told her abruptly. "Any other pets?"

"Just my dog, Sasha. She's a Saint Bernard."

Unexpected laughter surged through Morgan. "A big old Saint Bernard with a delicate name like Sasha?"

His laughter feathered across her, and Laura managed a painful smile. "She's very dainty for a Saint Bernard, Mr. Ramsey."

Morgan liked Laura's fighting spirit. "Call me 'Morgan.' We might as well be on a first-name basis. Okay, lady, I'll take care of your menagerie. You just lie back, sleep and get better."

She heard his footsteps retreating. "Morgan?"

He halted at the door. "Yes?"

"Are you sure you want to do this?"

Looking at her soft mouth and listening to her husky voice snapped the tension he'd held in check since this morning. "Yeah, I'm very sure, Laura. You don't leave a wounded comrade stranded. You're stuck with me."

She mustered a small smile. "Okay. Thanks..."

Pulling the door open, Morgan glanced back over his shoulder. "It's one o'clock. I'll be back tonight at visiting hours to report on your household."

"Tonight, then." Laura heard the door shut quietly, and the room suddenly seemed very lonely. Morgan Ramsey's larger-than-life presence was gone, and so was the confidence she'd felt while he was there with her. He'd made the pain go away, too. Touching her bandages gingerly, she prayed with all her heart that the blindness wasn't permanent. Exhaustion eroded her already unraveling emotions, and as she slid into a deep, healing sleep, she wondered what Morgan would think of her small home.

The rain drizzled to a halt as Morgan drove up the narrow asphalt driveway of Laura Bennett's home. The two-story brick home sat back off the road, surrounded by thirty-foot-tall, blossoming pink and white rhododendron bushes. Morgan shut off the red sports car's engine and leaned back to take stock of the house. Three large elm trees towered above it, their branches like arms creating a protective umbrella over the roof. The white shutters at each of the many windows gave the house a quaint appearance, reminding him of the neatly kept homes in the English countryside.

Not able to put his finger on what he felt about the place, Morgan slowly unfolded himself from the small car. The MR2 was excellent for someone of normal size, but his six-foot-five frame and two hundred thirty pounds of tightly packed muscle didn't fit well in such confines.

A white picket fence enclosed Laura's small front yard, he noted, and tulips, hyacinths and yellow daffodils crowded along the front of the house, creating a rainbow of welcoming color. A slight smile thawed the line of Morgan's mouth. The fairy-tale exterior of the house reflected the story-book innocence that flowed from its owner. An idealistic statement, Morgan decided, putting the key in the front door and opening it.

The cold nose of a Saint Bernard poked through the crack in the door, and Morgan spoke gently to the dog, not wanting to startle her. The animal stood in the entrance, enthusiastically wagging her thick brown-and-white tail. A grin crossed Morgan's mouth as he entered and shut the door behind him. Sasha was small for a Saint. He allowed her to sniff at him all she wanted, using the interlude to inspect Laura's residence.

The fairy-tale effect was even more pronounced inside the house. Filmy ruffled white curtains hung over each window, heightening the femininity of the residence. There were pots of African violets on a number of windowsills and sitting on Queen Anne tables, plus a variety of lush greenery in each corner.

"Antique and otherworld," Morgan said. He felt Sasha's pink tongue adoring his hand. Leaning over, he patted her large, broad skull, noting the dancing lights in her huge brown eyes.

"You're just like your mistress, aren't you?" he demanded. "Trusting and naive." Not a good combination for this world, Morgan thought as he moved through the lavender carpeted rooms. The wallpaper was ivory colored, with tiny violets sprinkled across it.

No doubt Laura loved the Victorian era, a very romantic period. He shook his head, unable to get her beautiful blue eyes out of his mind.

The baby robin was in a small cage sitting on the kitchen countertop. Morgan scowled down at the bird, who had a wide yellow beak, sparkling black eyes and a cheep that filled the room.

"Hungry, huh?" He turned to go to the refrigerator, and nearly tripped over Sasha. The dog gazed up at him lovingly and Morgan swallowed his reprimand. The kitchen was sunny, with two walls of windows that overlooked the backyard. Morgan wasn't surprised that the yard resembled an English garden in every sense of the word. He could see the round, rectangular and square areas formed by bricks. There were probably different herbs or flowers in each area, he thought, noting green shoots. Opening the door to the refrigerator, Morgan bent down and spotted a carton with "worms" written on the side of it.

The robin hopped onto his finger the moment he put the carton into the cage, and grudgingly Morgan fed the bird a couple of worms. Sated, she sat contentedly on his finger afterward, emitting contented little cheeps.

"Wish it took so little to satisfy everything else in life," Morgan told the robin, putting her back on the perch in the cage. Sasha whined at the back door, wanting out. Morgan shut the wire door to the cage and walked over, allowing the Saint Bernard out into the enclosed yard.

Drawn to explore the entire house, Morgan tried to ask himself why. His world consisted of minding his own business. The men of the Legion lived only in the present, never the past—or the future. But Laura haunted him, like a beautiful dream after he'd awakened. She was like elusive fog that disappeared when the sun shone directly on it. He snorted softly as he walked down the hall and into another room. Maybe he was dreaming and was really on a jet back to France.

Standing at the entrance to a room, he realized that this was her office. A computer terminal sat on a large, elegantly carved cherry desk. Floor-to-ceiling bookshelves lined two of the walls. Morgan wandered over to the terminal and looked at several papers beside it. Frowning, he picked them up.

" 'The Buildup of Soviet Military Power' by L. Bennett," he muttered. He stood reading the carefully typed ten-page manuscript. "I'll be damned." His fairy-tale Laura was a technical writer. Obviously a good one, because she had an insider's knowledge of Soviet hardware.

He dropped the manuscript back on the desk and turned around. Looking at the rows of books, he noticed that two of them had been written by her. Taking the first off the shelf, he saw that the book dealt with tactics and strategy in World War II. The second was a detailed account of all the major battles during the Korean War.

Scratching his head, he put both books back on the shelf. She was some kind of military expert. How?

Most women had little interest in that topic, much less any expertise in it. "Laura Bennett, you're one hell of an interesting person," he said, leaving the room.

She was going to need a robe and some other items for her stay in the hospital. He had to find her bedroom.

When he did he was speechless. Laura's bedroom was a Victorian fantasy. He stood at the threshold of the large room, staring at the flowery print covering the canopied bed. The elegantly carved bureau shouted her refined taste. A bowl of dried lavender flowers filled the room with a clean scent. He entered the dark-blue carpeted room, pulling himself out of the dreamy state the room induced. White French doors concealed two walk-in closets. Feeling as though he were trespassing, Morgan opened the closet door and found three cotton gowns hanging there. They were delicately embroidered with flowers, with pastel ribbons at the neckline and puffed sleeves. He folded the gowns carefully, located a small suitcase and placed them and other necessary items in it.

Then, going to the back door, he called Sasha. The Saint Bernard bounded back into the house, panting happily. Grinning, Morgan reached down, patting her thick, broad head. "I'll be back a little later to make sure you don't get housebound, big girl."

Morgan lingered in the front room, suitcase in hand. The feeling of serenity in the clean, neatly kept house was overwhelming. He wanted to relax, kick off his shoes and stretch out. Sasha came and sat, ladylike, at his side, her pink tongue lolling out the side of her mouth, her brown eyes sparkling. Morgan laughed harshly at himself as his shoulders, usually tense and drawn up, relaxed of their own accord. What kind of magic did Laura Bennett weave? He gazed around at the transparent draperies gracing each window. Laura's home was the direct opposite of what he was used to: a bunk in a sterile barracks with a highly polished floor and no sign of individual expression. Life in the Legion was hard and demanding. This house mirrored the opposite: softness and gentleness. With a sigh, he told the dog goodbye and reluctantly closed the front door.

The next order of business was to find a nearby hotel. And then he'd have to wait until eight o'clock. Suddenly Morgan found himself restless, wanting to talk at length with Laura, to explore this intriguing young woman.

Laura sensed Morgan's arrival. The door to her private room had opened and closed a number of times previously, but somehow she knew it was him.

"Morgan?"

He halted at the foot of her bed, thinking she looked a bit better than last time. "How did you know?"

Nervously Laura made a gesture with her hand. "Just a feeling around you."

"So," he murmured, bringing the suitcase near her bed and sitting down in a chair, "you're intuitive on top of everything else."

His voice feathered through her, easing her anxiety over her blindness. Laura released a sigh and sat back against several pillows that had been arranged for her earlier. "What's that supposed to mean?"

Hungrily Morgan absorbed her delicate beauty. "It was a compliment. Your home reflects you."

She grinned slightly. "Ann teases me unmercifully about my house. She calls it Sleeping Beauty's Castle."

"I like your place." Morgan caught the sadness in his tone and tried to cover it up. "There's a romantic Victorian aspect to you."

But Laura had caught the sadness, too. She quelled her urge to ask him about the source of his grief. "I love that era. Did you see my leather-bound volumes by Victorian authors in my office?"

She was like sunlight, Morgan decided, warming beneath her honeyed voice, which was breathless with enthusiasm. Her blond hair had been washed and now hung in graceful abandon around her small shoulders. "Yeah, I saw your library." He rubbed his jaw. "I also saw a manuscript on your desk about Soviet hardware."

All Laura's fears began to erode in Morgan's presence. He'd think her foolish if she confided that he made her feel safe, as if everything about this experience were going to turn out positively. "You don't miss much, do you?"

"Not when my life can depend on it."

Laura tilted her head, assimilating his brusque answer. It was on the tip of her tongue to ask him about his frequently military references, but she decided to wait. "I make a living writing books and articles for the military establishment," she explained, then wrinkled her nose. "I know it's probably strange for a woman to be in that line of business, but I find it fascinating."

"Oh?"

She rested her hands on her blanketed lap. "I guess my fascination started because my adoptive father was in the marine corps."

Tension thrummed through Morgan, blips of his past flashing before his mind, as they always did in such moments. Scowling, he said, "Marine corps?"

"Yes. Dad was killed in 1970 in Saigon, during the closing days of the Vietnam conflict."

"I'm sorry," he muttered. "A lot of good men died over there at that time." The pain in his chest widened. His past, which had haunted him daily since he'd regained his memory, loomed like an ugly, festering sore before him.

"He believed in what he was doing, Morgan. Dad always believed in fighting for what he felt was right. I was raised around the military and found it interesting from a psychological viewpoint."

"So you were weaned on a military tradition. What about your adoptive mother?"

Laura gestured briefly with her hand. "She died in 1975 in a car accident."

"So now you're alone."

"It's not so bad." Laura managed a brave smile. "Except for times like this when I can't see."

Morgan wanted to get to another topic besides war. All it did was dredge up the faces of ghosts that stalked him nightly. "How are you feeling?"

"Better." *Much better since you're here,* Laura wanted to add, but squelched the urge. Lightly she touched her bandages. "Everyone's positive that when the swelling goes down, I'll be able to see again."

Morgan wanted to reach out and run his fingers down her long, elegant hand. "I've got a hunch you'll see."

"I hope so...I mean, my livelihood depends on my sight, Morgan."

To hell with it. Morgan leaned over and captured her hand. Her fingers were damp and cool. "No one's going to turn your life inside out," he promised her.

His hand was callused and warm, and Laura released a shaky breath. "I'm scared, Morgan. Scared to death. What if I don't see again? How am I going to write? How will I be able to interview? I mean, I spend half my life at the Pentagon, going through tons of files in the basement complex, looking for unclassified material for my articles and books."

He placed both his hands on hers. "Now listen to me, Laura, that isn't going to happen."

With a little laugh of desperation, Laura said, "God, I hope not. But bad things happen to good people, no matter what our intent was at the time."

Morosely Morgan agreed. "Yeah, bad things do happen to innocent people. You just have to be at the right place at the wrong time." As he had been on Hill

164 with his company of men seven years ago. As Laura had been for him today....

"I know so little about you, and yet I feel I've known you forever," Laura said softly. Removing her hands from his, she lay back against the pillows, her voice lowering with feeling. "When I first saw you across that roadway, I thought you were a mercenary. You looked so hard and tough. And that scar on your face made me think you were a soldier. But now... Well, you're far more caring than I'd first thought." She shook her head. "Just goes to show, you can't judge any book by its cover."

Reluctantly Morgan allowed her to reclaim her hands. "I've got a face that was rearranged by a Mack truck," he jested, trying to tease her out of her fear of being permanently blind.

"No! I didn't mean it that way," Laura said quickly. "You're far from ugly." Heat flowed into her neck and cheeks, and she knew she was blushing. "You have character. Every line has a story behind it. I'd much rather look at a face that's interesting than one that's got nothing on it."

Morgan chuckled. "Then you're going to like old age, lady. Everyone gets wrinkles by that time. I just got some of mine a little early, that's all."

She laughed with him. "Thanks for letting me walk out of the noose I prepared for myself."

"No harm done," Morgan assured her. "I look at this mug every morning when I shave, and so far I haven't broken too many mirrors."

His humor stirred her heart. He was always casti-
gating himself in some small way. "Morgan, you
haven't told me anything about yourself. If you're
going to be stuck with me for a while, I'd like to know
something about you."

With her military background and expertise Laura
would most likely know about his company being
slaughtered in 1970. Maybe it was just as well that she
was temporarily blind—that way she couldn't possibly identify him. With time, though, he was afraid
Laura would put two and two together. And he
couldn't have that happen. Not ever. No, he'd stay
with her long enough to make sure she was going to be
fine, and then he'd disappear back into Europe to his
other life. There was no alternative.

Laura took his silence as a reply. "I don't mean to
be snoopy," she began awkwardly.

"Sorry," Morgan muttered, "I was thinking about
something else."

"There's an accent to your speech. Are you from a
foreign country?"

Her ability to pick up little things like that shouldn't
surprise him, but it unnerved him. "I'm American,
but I live in France." It wasn't a lie, but it wasn't the
total truth, either. "For the past six years, I've been
putting my engineering skills to work for the French."

"An engineer," Laura marveled. "I was right. You
looked as if you could build things. Your hands are
square and large, and you looked as if you get a lot of
physical exercise."

Damn, she didn't miss much at all. "Right on all accounts. I build bridges." That was true, but he also dug ditches, canals and roads wherever the Legion wanted them.

"You're a man with wanderlust in his heart, always on the move."

Morgan squirmed because he didn't want to lie to her. "I do travel around," he said. "I've got enough foreign countries under my belt to last me a lifetime."

"Do I hear longing in your voice?" Laura asked. "Maybe you want to settle down and get some good home cooking and a family atmosphere for a bit."

He laughed, staring down at his scarred, callused hands. "Yeah, I dream about that every so often." Just as he wondered daily how his father and mother were doing down in Clearwater. The itch to pick up a phone and call them was excruciating. But Morgan didn't want to renew their heartbreak over his disappearance. Seven years had healed their grief. He didn't want to add to it now.

"I'm not such a bad cook," Laura hinted wryly. "If you help me in the kitchen, I can promise you some great home-cooked meals."

"I haven't had a decent meal in a long time," Morgan said fervently. He couldn't get that house out of his mind, or her beautiful bedroom. His vivid imagination was torturing him again, and he savagely slammed a lid on his needs. His dreams had died in 1970. There was no future for him. Ever.

Laura smiled gently. "You sound like a man starved for a little bit of home life."

Reluctantly Morgan rose. "I'm not going to answer on the grounds that it might incriminate me," he teased her, watching her lips move into a smile that touched his cold, aching heart.

"You're leaving?"

She must have heard him get up from the chair. "For being temporarily blind, you don't miss much, do you?"

Disappointed that he was going, Laura tried to mask her reaction. "Blame it on my dog ears. My parents always told me I was supersensitive to everything. I guess it's true."

Morgan reached over and patted her shoulder. "You wear it well. Look, I brought you a suitcase with some items you'll probably want while you're here in the hospital. I'll get a nurse to take care of unpacking them for you."

His touch on her shoulder was hesitant, almost shy, and Laura's senses told her that Morgan, despite his size and harshly carved face, was a gentle man underneath. "Thank you for everything, Morgan."

He walked to the door, taking one last glance at her. She looked like a waif in that dreary light-blue hospital gown. "You just get a good night's sleep. I'll go home and check on your pets. Then I'll be at the Grand Hotel. The nurses' station will have my phone number in case you need me."

Fear started to stalk her once more, and Laura tried to swallow it. "When will I see you again?"

Her mouth was delicious, but the corners were pulled in, as if she were experiencing either pain or fear. Morgan shrugged. "Considering I'm the guy who caused you to be in this predicament, I wouldn't think you'd want to see much of me too often."

"No...please, come back soon. Visiting hours start at eleven in the morning," Laura blurted. She compressed her lips, realizing that she sounded like a frightened little girl incapable of caring for herself. "I mean—" she rubbed her brow, the ache beginning again "—it gets lonely here, and I miss Robby and Sasha so much...."

"I understand," Morgan said quietly. He forced himself to open the door, instead of walking back over to her bed and enfolding her in his arms. Right now she needed a little care. That was what he was best at: caring. It came naturally to him. "I'll be here at eleven, then. That's a promise."

Chapter Three

I t's final, Dr. Taggert, I'm leaving."

Morgan stood in the open doorway of Laura's hospital room, listening to her raised voice. Taggert was standing at her bedside, an agitated look on his face.

"I'm glad you've arrived, Mr. Ramsey," the doctor muttered.

Laura turned her attention from the physician. "Morgan?"

He allowed the door to shut, painfully aware of the desperation in her tone. "It's me. What's going on?" Halting on the other side of her bed, he was surprised as Laura lifted her hand, trying to make contact with him. He took her hand firmly. Her fingers were icy cold.

"Morgan, I've made a decision," Laura said, speaking rapidly because she didn't want the doctor to interrupt. "I had a terrible night's sleep here. I feel good enough to leave. I need my home in order to heal." Her grip on him tightened. "Please take me home. I told Dr. Taggert I'd sign the release papers."

Automatically Morgan soothed her by stroking her hand. "Take it easy, Laura." He lifted his gaze to the physician, who was standing with crossed arms, a scowl deepening on his brow. "Doctor, is it safe for her to leave this soon?"

"She ought to stay here for at least forty-eight hours—for observation after any kind of head injury," he muttered defiantly. "That trauma to her head could cause a hemorrhage. She should remain at least another day so we can make sure that isn't going to happen."

Laura's nostrils flared. "Morgan, the X-rays on my hard head came back without any sign of a concussion!"

"It's only twenty-four more hours, Ms. Bennett."

"Morgan," Laura pleaded huskily, "will you take me home?"

"Yeah, hold on just a minute." He directed his attention back to Taggert. "She's obviously upset at having to stay, Doctor. And some people recuperate better in a familiar setting." He ought to know. Six months in a hospital bed in Japan had nearly driven him crazy while he'd recovered from his massive wounds. He understood Laura's need to get out of these sterile confines.

Scratching his head, Taggert walked toward the door. "If she insists on going home, she shouldn't be left alone."

"Think you can stand me underfoot for twenty-four hours?" he asked Laura.

"Yes." She fought to keep the wobble out of her voice. "Just let me go home, Morgan. You know what I need...."

He squeezed her hand, then placed it back in her lap. "I do," he agreed quietly. "Okay, Doctor, set things in motion. Ms. Bennett is going home."

Shrugging, Taggert pulled open the door. "Fine. A nurse will be down shortly with the forms to sign and a wheelchair."

Releasing a sigh, Laura sagged back against the pillows. "Thank you, Morgan. I'm sorry you had to walk in on our argument."

He grinned. "That's all right. I've been in a few crossfires before and managed to survive them."

"I knew you'd understand. I slept terribly last night, and I'm a grouch today. My head's fine. It's just my silly eyes." She made a graceful gesture with her hand. "My home is everything to me. It's safety. It's peace. Here I can't do anything except lie in bed. I feel so damned helpless!"

Morgan reached over and massaged her left shoulder gently. "Calm down, my flighty swan, I'll take you home."

His touch was firm and Laura relaxed the instant his hand rested on her shoulder. "I'm sorry to be such a pain in the rear. You probably think I'm—"

"You're not being unreasonable, Laura. I spent a lot of months in a hospital many years ago, and I almost went crazy. I wanted to go home, too, but I couldn't. I know how you're feeling. There's no apology needed. Okay?"

"Okay," Laura whispered. Rallying, she reached up, finding his hand and holding it between hers. "Thanks. At least when I get home, I can get up and move around or work on my article."

"Whoa, one thing at a time. Let's see how it feels just to get up and walk around. You took a severe bump to your head. You might get dizzy."

He was right, Laura conceded. "I never realized how much I disliked hospital environments until last night," she grumped. "You're right. I'll take it one step at a time."

Already color was coming back into her pale cheeks. He wanted to lean over and brush that slope of cheek to find out if Laura was as soft as she appeared to be. Morgan put a clamp on the simmering desires that automatically surfaced whenever he was around her.

"Morgan?"

"Yes?"

"Did you sleep well last night?"

He grinned. "No, I had a lousy night's sleep." He always did, but he didn't want to say that.

"Look, I know it's terribly awkward for you, having to stay at my house one night just to play babysitter. We barely know each other, but I trust you."

"I think I'll manage to sleep under your roof," he said dryly.

"You don't mind?"

"No." In all honesty he was looking forward to sleeping in a real home.

The nurse came in with a clipboard holding several papers. Another nurse followed her. For the next fifteen minutes, Morgan was busy taking instructions on how to dress Laura's eyes twice daily and bandage them. She signed the forms with his help, and then a wheelchair was ushered into the room.

Morgan gripped her hand. "You ready to fly this place?" he asked.

Eagerly Laura threw off the covers, exposing the long cotton nightgown. "Just get me my chenille robe and we're gone." Right now all she wanted was home.

"Sasha!" Laura cried, throwing her arms awkwardly around the whining Saint Bernard. Laughter bubbled up in her throat as she hugged her dog affectionately.

Morgan stood back, suitcase in one hand, and quietly closed the front door behind him. Sunlight poured through the east windows, illuminating the living room, alive with life. Laura looked tiny in comparison to the huge, tail-wagging Saint, who panted happily and whined a joyous greeting to her mistress.

Laura stood, her hand moving outward, connecting with Morgan's. He was always there, somehow sensing when she needed his help. "Oh, Morgan, it's so wonderful to be home!" Her voice trembled, but she didn't care.

He smiled, holding her hand more firmly. "I know... Come on, let's get you to your bedroom."

"No, take me to the bathroom, will you? I want to fill the tub with orange blossom bubble bath and soak off this hospital smell!"

Her enthusiasm was infectious, and he chuckled. "Okay, little swan, let's fly to your bath so you can smell like oranges instead of antiseptic."

Morgan led her into the long, rectangular bathroom that had a green carpet and sunny wallpaper covered with white and yellow daisies. He marveled over his and Laura's innate ability to work as a team without any conversation. Laura started filling the bath and poured the bubble liquid into the water, the scent of orange blossoms filling the air. He left and went to her bedroom. In no time he had chosen a pair of tan slacks, a pink blouse and lingerie for her to wear after her bath. Placing them on the vanity, he shut the door and left.

It was past noon and he was hungry. Walking out to the kitchen, he fed the noisy baby robin, then attended to the details of a lunch for himself and Laura. Sasha sat at his feet, thumping her thick tail, as he made peanut butter sandwiches. "No," he told the dog, "this other sandwich is for your mistress."

Sasha tilted her head, whining.

"Oh, all right...." Morgan threw her a slice of bread and watched it disappear inside her cavernous mouth. "Good thing you're friendly. I'd hate to get bitten by the set of choppers you've got," Morgan muttered, and went back to making lunch.

Laura emerged half an hour later. Using her hand, she followed the hallway wall until it intersected with the kitchen. "Are you in here?" she asked.

Morgan looked up from where he was sitting in the sunny breakfast nook. "Yes. Hold on, I'll help you over to the table."

Laura held up her hand. "No, stay there. I've got to get around on my own, Morgan." Smiling, she added, "I feel a hundred and ten percent better! Did I button this blouse right, or is it hanging at an angle?"

He got to his feet, quietly coming to her side, just in case she stumbled on her way across the kitchen. "You look fine." Hell, she looked breathtakingly beautiful. She had taken off the bandage and washed her hair, then replaced the dressing afterward. Her golden hair hung damply around her shoulders. The fragrance of orange blossoms filled his nostrils as he remained close to her. The pale-pink blouse was excruciatingly feminine, the ruffles around her slender neck emphasizing her delicate beauty. The mobility of her lips entranced him, and Morgan felt heat uncurling deep within him. A gnawing hunger made him all too aware of how she affected him.

Making contact with the wooden chair, Laura pulled it out and sat down. "Success!" she declared, laughing.

"You're doing fine," Morgan congratulated her. "Here's lunch." He placed the plate with the sandwich in front of her. "I made some coffee. You want some?"

Famished, Laura picked up the sandwich. "Yes, please." She smelled it. "Peanut butter. One of my favorites. Thanks for making it."

Heat nettled Morgan's face as he poured coffee into the dainty china cup decorated with pansies. Her gratefulness made him feel as if he'd given her the most beautiful gift in the world. "I'm afraid my skills as a cook are lacking, Laura."

"Why do you always belittle what you do, Morgan?"

Settling back at the table, opposite her, he scowled. "What do you mean?"

Laura placed the half-eaten sandwich on the plate in front of her, hearing the carefully veiled pain in his voice. "You're always cutting yourself down in some way," she murmured. "That self-deprecating humor isn't deserved."

Pushing the cup around on the saucer, Morgan scowled. "Yes, it is," he said, and let it go at that. One look at her face, however, and he realized she wasn't going to let him off the hook that easily. "You're too damn good at being a writer," he griped.

"What do you mean?"

"You pick up nuances in people."

"Does it make you uncomfortable?"

"Yes."

She chuckled. "Why? Because you have something to hide?"

He winced. She was close to the truth. "There isn't a human being alive who doesn't have some secret," he parried.

Laura warmed to their conversation. He was so easy to talk to. "And how many secrets are you carrying, Morgan Ramsey?" she teased.

The china cup looked small in comparison to Morgan's darkly tanned hands. "More than I'd like," he admitted hesitantly.

Sobering, Laura leaned forward. "I'm a great secret keeper, Morgan. Lord knows, when I interview the generals and admirals over at the Pentagon, they sometimes slip and tell me things that could never go into print."

He eyed her. "You're just a regular Pandora's Box, huh?"

"You could say that. I've been rubbing shoulders with the Pentagon people for the past seven years, and they've come to trust me. I hold what they say in confidence." Laura straightened and grinned. "And those things go to the grave with me."

Frowning, he muttered, "Well, you came too damn close to the grave the other day by saving my neck."

"I wouldn't have had it any other way, Morgan."

The sudden quaver in Laura's voice sent a wave of yearning through him. He stared hard at her. There was an underlying strength to her, despite her innate femininity. "I believe you," he whispered.

Laura detected an opening in the wall that so thoroughly protected Morgan Ramsey. "When I first came here after graduating from college, I rented this house." She gestured around the room with her hand. "I fell in love with it. At the time my dad was over in Vietnam, and I sent him pictures of every room." Her voice grew warm with love. "He was so excited for me. We traded letters for six months on how I was going to decorate each room. Of course, Mom got in on it, too. We'd send him swatches of material, wallpaper samples and photos from magazines of the furniture I someday wanted to be able to afford." She picked up the cup, sipping the cooling coffee. "I think my letters and dreams for this house helped my dad. It was a piece of reality from a world other than the one he fought in daily." Laura shook her head. "I still have all his letters...."

A lump formed in Morgan's throat. "Letters from home meant everything to me—" He caught himself. Damn!

"You were in Vietnam?" Of course, he would have been the right age.

A frown furrowed his brow. "Yeah, I was over there." The words came out harsh and clipped.

Biding time because she heard his anger and pain, Laura drank her coffee. She'd met many veterans who didn't want to discuss what had happened to them over there, and she felt Morgan was like that, too. Gently she steered the conversation back to her father. "The living room was Dad's idea—the colors and the fabric. And so was the kitchen." Fondly she laughed. "At the time we were playing this silly game, I really didn't have any money for redecorating. But that didn't matter. At least it offered Dad some sanity while he was over there. And Mom didn't worry as much, because she had something to do, too."

Morgan could no longer sit still. The ghosts were rising in his memory again—the anger and frustration along with them. He paced slowly around the kitchen. "So how did you manage to get this house bought and decorated?"

Leaning back, Laura sensed he'd moved away from the table. There was a new and different energy around him, and she felt his tension. "Dad was killed in a rocket attack in the seventh month of his tour. What I didn't realize was that he'd taken out nearly half a million dollars in insurance before he left for Vietnam, just in case he did get killed. My mother and I found out about it when the lawyer read his will to us three weeks later." She rose, picking up her cup and saucer and moved carefully to the drainboard. "So I bought this house instead of renting it, and Mom and I took each room, just as we'd planned it in our letters to Dad, and decorated."

Morgan stood in the center of the kitchen, staring at Laura. There was a sad smile on her lips. "It must have been hard," he said, his voice hoarse.

"No, just the opposite really. I cried a lot, because he was a wonderful father and friend to me. So did Mom. But wallpapering and painting each room, then buying the furniture helped us expend our grief and get over his passing." She patted the drainboard. "This home reflects the love we had as a family. That's why I love it so much." She gave him a shy look. "Maybe now you can understand why I wanted to come home from the hospital. I work through trauma better here than anywhere else."

Morgan tried to fight his need to hold her, but he walked up to her. Gently placing his hands on her shoulders, he looked down at her. "You're like this home," he told her, his voice rough with emotion, "warm, caring and beautiful. Your parents gave you a lot of love, and it shows in many ways."

It felt so natural to lean her head against his chest and rest for just a moment. Laura sighed as Morgan's arms slid around her shoulders, drawing her gently against him. "Right now, I don't feel very strong, Morgan."

She fitted against his tall frame, Morgan thought, a willow in comparison to an oak. The fragrance that was hers alone filled his nostrils. He fought to keep his touch light and comforting, not intimate, as he wanted. "You're stronger than you think," he told Laura gruffly, his mouth near her ear. Caressing her back with his hands, he felt the firm softness of her flesh beneath the silk blouse. If he didn't step back, he'd kiss her, and that wouldn't be right. The timing was all wrong—as usual.

Laura felt bereft as Morgan gently disengaged himself. "I—I'm sorry. I shouldn't have—"

"Shh," Morgan remonstrated, keeping one hand on her upper arm as she swayed. "That's one of many things I like about you, Laura Bennett—your ability to show your feelings. If you're feeling weak, you lean. If you're feeling strong, you get feisty." He grinned. "You're one hell of a woman, did you know that?"

She shook her head, forcing herself to retreat from him. Shaken by the unexpected contact, Laura found herself wanting more. "No, you're wrong," she whispered, her voice strained, "you're the one who's special."

Snorting vehemently, Morgan got busy and cleared the rest of the dishes from the table. "I'm special all right," he growled. *Just ask the press or the Pentagon. They'll tell you all about me.* He glanced at her after setting the dishes in the sink. Her lips were pursed, as if she were deep in thought. All this seemed like a fevered dream. This house that throbbed with life, the beauty and generosity of Laura, were all baubles being dangled cruelly in front of him and his harsh existence. If she found out he was Morgan Trayhern, the traitor, she'd scorn him. Sadness flowed through him, effectively squelching the fires of longing for her. Morgan hadn't fully realized just how tough it would be to stay around Laura. Somehow he'd have to contain his unraveling emotions. Maybe by tonight things would settle into a routine, and he'd be able to control the feelings that Laura brought to brilliant, yearning life within him. Maybe...

"The fire feels wonderful," Laura murmured, sitting with her back to the fireplace. "April nights are always chilly in D.C." Sasha lay directly in front of the fire, snoring fitfully.

Morgan sat nearby in an overstuffed chair. He marveled at Laura's hair, golden threads highlighted by the fire. She had dressed for bed and was wearing a long white cotton gown, her lavender chenille robe wrapped about her slender body. "You give April nights a new meaning," he admitted, his voice deeper than usual.

She drew her knees up, resting her cheek on them, a soft smile on her lips. "It sounds as if in your business you spend a lot of time outdoors. I imagine a quiet night like this *is* different for you."

The magazine in Morgan's lap was a poor substitute for staring like a starving wolf at Laura. He was disgusted with himself, taking advantage of her blindness by watching her for minutes at a time. It wasn't as if he couldn't have a woman if he wanted. That wasn't the issue at all. The issue was Laura and her Dresden doll delicacy, her graceful motions with her hands, that heart-grabbing laughter that made him want to drag her into his arms and crush her against him, never letting her go.

Morgan cleared his throat. "I do spend a lot of time outside," he admitted. Did she hear the longing in his voice? God, he hoped not. She trusted him completely, and he wouldn't reward that trust by letting her know of his insatiable need for her.

Lulled by the peace swirling gently between them, Laura confessed, "When I saw you standing there in the rain at the airport, I sensed this terrible tragedy and loneliness in you, Morgan. That scar on your face..."

Uncomfortable, he placed the magazine on the coffee table. "I'd just gotten some bad news that morning," he said gruffly.

"That scar...did you get it in Vietnam?" Somehow Laura sensed that the suffering surrounding Morgan stemmed from that time in his life. The need to get to the real him, the man she sensed beneath all that weight he carried on his powerful shoulders, was forcing her to ask deeply personal questions.

Automatically Morgan's fingers went to the ridge of the scar, and he scowled. "Yeah, I got it there."

"Tell me how?"

His stomach knotted. If Laura had been pushy or curious, it would have been easy to tell her to mind her own business, but the quaver in her voice unstrung him, and he leaned back, closing his eyes. "I got it in hand-to-hand combat. My company and I were led into a trap and we had to defend a hill," he said in a low, hard voice.

"My God," she whispered. Slowly she got up from her spot near the fireplace. Hand outstretched, she took small steps in the direction of where Morgan sat. Her lips parted as his fingers wrapped strongly around her arm and he guided her to the chair near him. She sat back down on the floor, nestled at his feet, her back against the chair. "I didn't mean to pry," she told him softly. "But you wear sadness around you like a good friend, Morgan." She took a deep breath and dove in. "We barely know each other, and I know your personal life isn't any of my business, but I just can't seem to help myself. If I'm being nosy, tell me to quit asking questions."

He lifted his hand, and noticed it was trembling. Laura's face was tilted in his direction, her lips parted, pleading. Stroking her hair, Morgan managed a tortured smile. "Sweet Laura," he said thickly, "your heart is pure, so you can see straight through a person." Her hair was clean, and the strands flowed like molten gold between his scarred fingers.

Her breath caught in her throat as his fingers trembled across her hair, again and again. "I don't need eyes to hear the pain in your voice, Morgan," Laura whispered. "I—there's something special we share. I can't define it, but it's there." She placed her hand on his knee, lifting her face more in his direction. "Something tragic happened to you yesterday morning. That's why you stepped off that curb without looking. Please, let me help, if I can...." She moistened her lips. "If nothing else, I'm a good listener, Morgan. And I care..."

Pain, like a volcano inside his chest, exploded violently within him. It seared his heart, soaring up into his throat, and he leaned forward, resting his cheek against the top of Laura's head ever so lightly, needing the comfort she offered. Without a word, he gripped her shoulders, simply holding her, his breathing ragged.

A little cry escaped Laura's lips, and she placed her arm around his shoulder. "Morgan, what is it? You're shaking."

Shutting his eyes tightly, he fought to find his voice. "This isn't real," he said gruffly. "None of this is real, especially you...."

His hands were splayed across her back, and Laura relaxed within them. Something was terribly wrong.

Blindly she groped with her hand, her fingers coming in contact with his face. She could feel the thick welt of the scar that ran the length of his face. "You're wrong," she said, her voice quavering. "This is all real, Morgan. Especially me. I can feel your pain.... Talk to me about it. Whatever it is, I can deal with it."

The desire to spill the horrible facts surrounding his life dealt him an almost lethal blow. Her fingers were warm against his chilled flesh. He fought the overpowering urge to tilt her face upward and crush those pleading lips beneath his mouth. His heart pounded erratically in his chest, and his breathing was harsh. "N-no," he whispered, "I can't."

"Can't or won't?" Laura asked, gently running her fingers across the scar.

If he didn't push her away, he'd take her, and Laura didn't deserve that. He released her slender form, keeping his hands on her shoulders as he drew away. "Both," he said thickly.

He'd been so close to allowing that awful load he carried to slide into her waiting arms. Laura swallowed her disappointment. She managed a small smile and lifted her hands so that they came to rest on his forearms. The tightly muscled power in them fairly vibrated through her fingertips. "From the moment I saw you, I knew you were special, Morgan."

A startled laugh broke from him. He gave her a gentle shake. "Special? You've got your priorities skewed, sweet swan."

She laughed softly. "Swan? Is that how you see me? Tall and skinny with my bird-size bones?"

Her laughter melted the wall of pain that threatened to engulf him. It was a miracle in itself, and Morgan stared down at her. "Yeah, you're a beautiful, graceful swan." He released her shoulders and picked up one of her wrists, turning it over carefully in his large hands. "You're tiny but mighty."

His touch was evocative, sending warming threads of yearning up Laura's arm, the heat flowing through her like an awakening river of molten lava. "So, you see my backbone of steel?" She ached to lean upward, find his mouth and kiss him.

"A beautiful spine and a set of small, but very strong shoulders," he murmured. All he had to do was lean forward—mere inches—to kiss her. He shut his eyes, fighting the overwhelming urge.

"Make me a promise, Morgan?"

He felt her hands tighten on his arms. "What?"

"You know I'm strong enough to hear anything you might tell me. Promise me that if you want to talk, you'll unload your burden on me?"

Smiling gently, he placed a chaste kiss on her wrinkled brow. "Sweet, guileless swan. Come on, you've had a long day, and it's time for bed."

Morgan's kiss had been fleeting. His mouth had been strong against her forehead, and Laura felt the heat escalate within her at his unexpected gesture. "I think you're right," she whispered. "This swan is ready to call it a night."

Chapter Four

Be quiet, you little beggar, or you'll wake up Laura," Morgan growled at the robin, who frantically cheeped in her cage. Morning sunlight cascaded through the green curtains at the windows. Rubbing his face tiredly, Morgan went through the motions of feeding the baby bird. Who could believe this almost featherless creature could cause such a ruckus?

Morgan knew he'd overslept. He'd been unable to sleep for a long time after his conversation with Laura by the fireplace. And then his sleep had been broken with nightmarish memories intermixed with Laura's haunting face dancing before him. Dressed in only a pair of pajama bottoms, Morgan enjoyed the feel of the sunlight against his upper body as he stood at the sink, feeding the robin her morning meal.

"I'll tell you what, little lady, you're lucky I put up with you."

"Morgan?"

He turned, hearing Laura's sleep-filled voice. His heart tightened in his chest as he took in her rumpled appearance. Sasha, who'd slept in her mistress's bedroom, wagged her tail in greeting as she ambled toward Morgan. Sometime during the night Laura's bandage had slipped off. Her blue eyes were incredibly large and thickly lashed. Dragging in a deep breath, he felt that same molten desire explode through him just as it had the night before.

"It's okay," he mumbled. "We both overslept and this little beggar was hungry."

Laura smiled and walked slowly toward Morgan's voice, her hand held out in front of her. "I heard Robby cheeping like crazy. I thought something was wrong," she offered huskily, finding the countertop and halting.

Laura's eyes were puffy with sleep, her hair mussed and framing her face. Morgan swallowed hard, putting the robin back in the cage. "She won't squawk for at least an hour. I stuffed her with four worms."

Laura chuckled and tried to smooth her hair away from her face. "Despite all your snarling and growling about feeding Robby, I really think you like her." Wildly aware of Morgan's overpowering masculinity, Laura sensed she was very close to him. Her dreams had been torrid, centering around her in Morgan's arms.

"You look beautiful just the way you are," Morgan said thickly. He placed the cage back against the wall and turned to her. The white cotton gown was wrinkled, the boat neck revealing her finely sculpted collarbones and emphasizing the smooth expanse of her throat. "And you're going to catch your death of cold if you don't get a robe."

"Oh, dear, I forgot to put it on." Laura pressed both hands to her cheeks, feeling heat steal into them. The gown she wore wasn't sexy in her mind, but she heard the longing in Morgan's tone. "I'm sorry," she began lamely. "I'm so used to padding around here alone in my gown when I get up in the morning."

Squeezing her upper arm, Morgan murmured, "Don't be. Hold on, I'll get the robe for you."

Laura turned toward the sunlight, reveling in the warmth enveloping her. In a minute, Morgan returned and helped her on with the chenille robe.

"Can you see anything yet?" Morgan asked, standing next to her, studying her flawless blue eyes. The pupils were huge and black.

Dejectedly Laura shook her head. "No—nothing." She bit down on her lower lip. "Morgan, what if Dr. Taggert is wrong? What if this isn't temporary?"

He heard the carefully concealed terror in her voice. "I learned a long time ago to live one day at a time, Laura. You do the same."

All her fears surfaced as Morgan's hand came to rest on her shoulder. "My livelihood depends on my being able to see. I've got three articles due at different magazines in the next two weeks. They're typed, but they need to be edited and then a final copy run off on the printer."

"One day at a time, little swan," Morgan urged, sliding his arm around her drawn shoulders. There was no reasoning around Laura, he realized with a pang as he drew her against him. She brought out so many withheld emotions in him, and he responded to them without even thinking. Giving her a quick squeeze and then releasing her, he said, "Let me make breakfast. You have your bath and get dressed. After we're done eating, I'll help you with those articles."

Laura turned, gripping his hand. "Oh, Morgan, would you?"

He smiled down into her eyes, which sparkled with renewed hope. "I'm not very good at typing, but we'll get them done. Let's go to your bedroom and figure out what you want to wear today. Then I'll whip up a breakfast of scrambled eggs and bacon."

"Well," Laura asked, sitting at her office desk, "what do you think of the first article?"

Morgan had brought another chair into the office and placed it next to hers. He'd finished reading the ten-page article on spy satellites. "Very good."

She caught the admiration in his voice. "I can almost hear you asking how a woman could know so much about something so complex, right?"

He grinned up at her. Laura had chosen to wear a pink long-tailed shirt that hung over her curved thighs and a pair of jeans. She had begged him to leave the bandages off her eyes, and he'd agreed. Her blond hair framed her face in a natural page boy, barely grazing her shoulders. The bangs fell softly across her brow, following the gentle slope of her eyebrows.

"No... I'm more impressed with *how* you got this kind of information. Isn't it classified?"

She chuckled. "No. I've got friends down at the Pentagon vaults where all the declassified material is kept. I practically live down there some days, reading through hundreds of pages of information, pulling out interesting tidbits and then compressing them into an article format."

"I'm impressed."

"Will you read the article back to me, sentence by sentence? That way I can listen to it and see if something needs to be changed or tightened up."

"Yeah, and I'll input the edits and then print out a final draft for you."

She reached out, her hand coming in contact with his chest instead of his arm. The tensile strength of his muscles sent a thrill through her. She moved her hand to find his arm, giving it a warm squeeze. "We work well as a team, don't we?"

"Since the beginning," Morgan agreed huskily, lost in the beauty of her eyes. Eyes that showed him the world in a frame of hope, not despair. Rousing himself from his discovery, he grabbed a pencil. "Okay, here comes the first sentence. If we're lucky, we'll be finished by noon.''

Morgan dawdled over the noontime meal of tuna salad sandwiches, sweet pickles and potato chips with Laura. The first article was completed. He couldn't recall the last time he'd had so much fun or laughed as hard as he had in that three-hour period. Between editing and the five phone calls that Laura had answered, the article had been revised and printed out to perfection.

Laura licked her fingers after finishing off a third sweet pickle. A new kind of excitement was growing inside her—a sweet euphoria she'd never felt before. It was all due to Morgan, she realized. The need to know more about him never left her. Picking up the paper napkin, she blotted her lips. Sasha sat by her chair, begging for another sweet pickle, a favorite food of hers.

"Every time you feed the robin, you act as if you don't like to do it," Laura noted. "Why?"

Disgruntled once again by her acute hearing and observation, Morgan said, "When I came home from the naval academy on leave for the first time, my sister, Aly, and I went out hunting together. Actually," he went on, frowning, "I was the one who wanted to hunt. Aly was happy just to tag along." He shook his head, a smile edging his mouth. "She was only twelve at the time and had missed her big brother, so she was like my shadow on that first leave."

Laura leaned forward, hearing the nostalgia in Morgan's voice. "It sounds as if Aly idolizes you."

He laughed softly. "Yeah. She was a great kid sister, always hanging around with Noah and me." Glancing up at Laura, he halted, realizing just how much he'd divulged about his past by naming his brother and sister. Would Laura piece things together? Judging from the tenderness in her eyes, Morgan guessed not, and slowly continued.

"I had this .22 caliber rifle I'd grown up with as a kid. My dad and I had gone deer hunting every fall for as long as I could remember. Aly didn't usually like to come with us because she hated to see anything killed. I'd taken the rifle along for the hell of it as we walked through this wooded grove. I wanted to keep up my proficiency shooting, so I was aiming at tree branches in the distance, not birds or animals." Morgan crumpled the napkin in his hands, staring down at the light-green tablecloth.

"I picked out a branch on one tree and fired. There was a robin's nest on it, hidden by leaves, and I hadn't realized it was there. The nest fell out of the tree. Aly ran over to it. When I got there, she was crying."

"Oh, Morgan," Laura whispered, sliding her hand outward, making contact with his. "I'm sorry."

He shrugged, the memory returning powerfully to him. "Two of the three baby robins were dead. The third one had a broken wing, and Aly gently picked it up. She thought we could save it, so I wrapped the bird up in my handkerchief to keep it warm for the walk back to the house.

"When we got home, Aly and I got a shoe box, made a little nest for the bird and kept it warm. She went outside with me to dig worms. I felt terrible, because I'd had no intention of killing anything," Morgan admitted.

Laura tightened her fingers around his. "Did the baby live?"

He sighed. "It died two days later. It must have had internal injuries. The bird should have survived with only a broken wing."

"You both must have been devastated."

Morgan took her hand between his, lightly tracing each of her long, artistic fingers. "Aly cried for hours after the baby died. All I could do was hold her and tell her I was sorry, that I hadn't meant to hurt the robin."

"She wasn't upset with you, was she?"

"No, not Aly. She's just as softhearted as you are."

Sniffing, Laura swallowed back her tears for Morgan's sake. He might misconstrue her compassion for pity. "Robby brings all those memories back to you, doesn't she?"

Looking over at the robin, who slept contentedly in the makeshift nest of grass in the cage, Morgan nodded. "Yeah, the little beggar brings it all back to me. Except maybe this time I won't kill it. Maybe she'll live despite me."

The urge to whisper his name and pull him into her arms was real. Instead Laura held his hand tightly. "Why do I get this feeling that you think everything you touch is somehow worse off?"

"Not much in my life has had a good ending, Laura," Morgan warned her darkly, getting up. "I don't have to stay in one place long before things turn to hell in a hand basket. Look at you. All you had to do was see me at an airport and you got injured saving my miserable neck."

"I don't believe it," Laura told him fervently. "You're a kind and good person."

"Tell that to the world," he growled, picking up the plates and taking them to the dishwasher. "Come on, let's get back to work on those last two articles."

Phone calls from well-wishers who had found out about her injury via the newspaper, and editors whom Laura had worked with, came in all afternoon. Some flowers arrived, and Morgan brought them into her office. Her enthusiasm over receiving the fragrant bouquet did nothing but remind him that he should have had the sensitivity to bring her some, too. By six o'clock, Morgan was in ill humor.

He got up and went to the kitchen to make them supper. His anger at the situation bred more frustration. What if she was blinded for life? He couldn't just leave her stranded. In his mind, no one who was loyal ever deserted. As he peeled the potatoes, he began to consider the possibility of staying stateside. He now knew he wasn't a CIA mole. So it didn't matter whether he signed up for another five-year stint with the French Foreign Legion or not.

Throwing the potatoes into a pot to boil, Morgan began collecting the vegetables from the refrigerator for a salad.

"Here, little beggar," he muttered, throwing the robin a piece of lettuce. The bird promptly climbed out of her nest in the bottom of the cage and gobbled up the greenery. Morgan grinned tightly, throwing her another piece. "Greedy little thing, aren't you?"

So was he, if he were honest with himself. He liked Laura a hell of a lot—and not for reasons of pity or owing her for saving his life. Looking around at the quiet kitchen, he was astonished, as he always was, by the peace that reigned within this home. Tearing up bib lettuce leaves and putting them in a large bowl, Morgan realized his newfound contentment was due to Laura.

And if Laura's sight came back in two weeks, what would he do? He released a long sigh, grabbing a carrot and methodically beginning to slice it into the bowl. With her background in military information, she'd recognize him sooner or later. Disgruntled, he found himself wanting to stay, but realized it was a stupid dream. This was still nothing more than a beautiful dream that would end very abruptly.

"Mmm, smells good, whatever you're cooking," Laura said, coming into the kitchen. She found a chair in the nook and sat down. "Can I help?"

"I've got chicken in the oven, and I'm working on a salad. Just sit there and look beautiful."

Smiling, Laura murmured, "I wish I could see your face, Morgan Ramsey, when you say that."

"Oh? Why?"

"To see if you're teasing me or if you mean it."

He grinned as he chopped up a scallion. "And if I did mean it, Ms. Bennett, what would you do, I wonder?"

"You're such a rogue," she said with a laugh, clapping her hands delightedly. "And too much of an officer and a gentleman to take unfair advantage of me."

Scowling, he scooped the scallion into the bowl. The tomato was next. "Not anymore."

Undaunted by his growling rejoinder, she sat, enjoying his presence. "So, you graduated from Annapolis as an officer?"

"Yes."

"Navy?"

"No . . . marine corps."

Her eyebrows moved upward. "That makes sense."

"What does?"

"When I saw you, you reminded me of a tough-as-nails soldier. The marine corps image suits you."

"That's over with now," he said in a clipped tone. Moving the bowl of salad to the table, he opened the silver drawer and pulled out the necessary utensils.

"What's the saying? You can take the boy out of the country, but you can't take the country out of the boy? I think that applies to you in a marine corps sense. You're still a marine at heart, Morgan."

"Probably." She'd never know that he used those skills to this very day.

"Were you a lieutenant in Vietnam?"

He placed the silverware on the table, his scowl deepening. "No, a captain."

"My dad was a major in the army. He had a company of men to command while he was in Vietnam. Did you?"

Morgan straightened, feeling the tension thrum through him. "Yeah, I had one hundred sixty men under my command."

She tilted her head, hearing raw anguish in his voice. "It's a terrible responsibility," Laura whispered. "And knowing you the way I do, I'll bet you cared deeply for each and every one of them."

"Let's get on another subject, Laura. I don't feel like discussing this one very much."

Laura winced at the anger in his voice. She placed her hands in her lap and bowed her head. "Sometimes I can put my foot in my mouth, Morgan...."

He'd seen her face go pale at his snarling order to drop the topic. Cursing himself, he went over and knelt in front of her, scooping up her hands in his. "I'm the one who should apologize," he muttered. "I didn't mean to rip your head off."

"No, it's okay. It's just that some of your mannerisms make me think of Dad. In some ways you're alike."

"A soldier is a soldier," he uttered tiredly. "The uniform may be different, but underneath it, we're all the same. Scared men just trying to do our jobs and uphold our responsibilities."

Murmuring Morgan's name, Laura pulled her hands out of his and slid them across his shoulders. "I feel you're like Dad. You may have been overresponsible, Morgan. Maybe you cared a little too deeply, a little too much.... That can leave an open wound in your heart and memory. Even to this day.''

He longed to lean forward and rest his head against Laura. The anguish of the past stared him in the face. ''One thing our family prides itself on is responsibility,'' he told her in a strained tone. ''We have a long military tradition of caring for those under our command. My men were more than numbers to me, Laura. More than just sets of dog tags.''

She threaded her fingers through his short black hair. ''I know,'' she whispered, ''I know....''

A cry lodged in Morgan's throat as she drew him forward. The softness of her fingertips across his neck and shoulders melted his resolve. He shut his eyes, burying his face against her small, warm body. As she wrapped her arms around his shoulders, he felt a shudder work its way up and out of him. She smelled so good, so fresh and clean, when his world consisted of little more than dirt, sweat and desert. He slid his arms around her small waist, aware of her diminutive size against his bulk and brawn. Yet she was strong in ways that he wasn't right now, and that knowledge shook Morgan to the core.

Closing her eyes, Laura pressed him against her, his head resting on her bosom. When she felt him shudder, she tightened her arms around him. ''Oh, Morgan, you're so strong for so many, and I know you're tired,'' she murmured against his hair. ''I understand that. My dad carried the same terrible weight on his shoulders for almost fifteen years. I saw what his care and concern did to him. Every man was like the son he never had. He knew their names, the names of their wives and children. And whenever one of them died, he wrote a long letter to the wife and family.'' She smiled weakly and caressed his hair. ''The war isn't that far away from you, either, is it? It's a living hell for you today, just as it was years ago.''

Morgan held her tightly, hearing the fluttering beat of her generous heart beneath his ear. Each stroke of her hand on his head eased a little more of the anguish he'd carried so long by himself. When he felt her lips press against his temple, he groaned. God, he had to get a hold on himself for her sake. He wanted to take Laura, right now. He wanted to love her with wild, hungry abandon and hear her cry out with pleasure. But he wouldn't drag her into his morbid, complicated life. There was no happy ending for them. No, he wasn't going to ruin one more life.

''Listen to me,'' Morgan commanded harshly, easing out of her arms. He saw huge tears in her lustrous blue eyes, and he winced. ''Don't open yourself up to me and my problems, Laura. Dammit, you've got enough worries without taking on mine.''

Taking a deep, unsteady breath, she nodded. ''It's my nature to get involved, Morgan. I was adopted, and my parents always said I was a fighter for the underdogs of the world.''

With his thumbs he wiped away the two tears that trailed down her cheeks. ''Then fight for someone who's worth fighting for. I'm not. The die was cast for me many years ago, little swan.''

Laura struggled to control her escaping feelings for him—feelings of desire, not pity. Just the roughened touch of Morgan's thumbs against her flesh made her ache to love him. There was some deep inner knowing within her that if she could get him to trust her, she could help him in so many ways.

Forcing a slight smile, she murmured, ''I guess I'm letting this trauma get to me.''

He caressed her hair. ''Yeah, a close call with death can make you do things you're sorry for later.''

She nodded, biting down on her lower lip. She wanted to say, *Making love with you, Morgan, would be the most right thing in the world for both of us.* But she didn't. Let him think what he wanted. He brought out all her instincts for nurturing, caring and loving. And every piece of information she'd dragged out of him thus far told her his life was a picture of terrible tragedy. Something had happened to his company in Vietnam. What?

Rising to his feet, Morgan left her side. Despite his pleading, he saw the stubborn set of her chin and the spark of defiance in her eyes. Still, those warming seconds in her arms did nothing but make him starved to explore Laura. All of her. . . .

''Tomorrow morning,'' Laura began, her voice low with emotion, ''Captain Jim Woodward from the marine corps is coming over. I'll interview him at ten.''

Morgan leaned against the counter, scowling. A marine officer. The chances of getting recognized increased a hundredfold. He couldn't risk it.

"No problem. I'll go back to my hotel and—"

"No, that's not what I meant." Why did Morgan always think he was unwanted? "If you could tape the session and run the recorder, it would be of immense help to me."

Shifting uneasily, Morgan grimaced. "Look, I don't want to butt into your personal life."

Laughing, Laura said, "Captain Woodward isn't part of my personal life. He's a long-time associate whom I frequently contact for marine corps articles, that's all." Then she shrugged. "To tell you the truth, I don't have a personal relationship right now. I've spent the past year working on the second of three military history books." She almost added that her engagement to Major Roarke Anderson, an air force pilot, hadn't worked out. He couldn't handle her independence or the fact that she was a celebrated author. But that was a year ago, and her heart had healed, leaving room for someone else. For Morgan, perhaps....

Stymied by her honesty, Morgan paced the room. "I just thought this guy meant something to you."

"Then you'll stay and help me? Please?"

Rubbing his chin, Morgan wondered if Woodward would recognize him. It was a chance he'd have to take. Besides, he was relieved to hear Laura was free of any personal entanglements. "Sure, no problem."

* * *

Morgan answered the door. It was exactly ten, and he was sweating, hoping like hell Woodward wouldn't recognize him. He opened the door to a tall, well-built officer in a tan marine corps uniform.

"The name's Ramsey," Morgan said. "Ms. Bennett is expecting you."

Woodward's green eyes narrowed slightly. He hesitated fractionally, then held out his hand. "Captain Jim Woodward."

Morgan shook the officer's hand. It was similar to his own—callused and strong. This man wasn't any desk sitter at the Pentagon. If he wasn't so worried about being recognized, Morgan thought he would like the officer. Part of it was Woodward's proud carriage, his fearless green eyes and the square set of his face. Another part was the confidence and power he radiated. At one time, Morgan remembered, he had, too. "Come in. Ms. Bennett is in her office. Because of her injury, I'll be assisting her today."

"Fine. I know where her office is," Woodward said, taking off his cap and placing it beneath his left arm.

Laura heard both men coming and sat expectantly in her office chair. Today she wore a teal-blue silk blouse and an ivory skirt and jacket—all business. She never appeared for an interview without wearing a suit. Nervously she kept her hands in her lap. Would Jim's discomfort over her blindness interfere with the forthcoming interview?

"Hey, tiger," Jim called from the door. "It's all over the Pentagon that you bumped your head and hurt yourself. How are you feeling?"

Relief swept through her that the two men got along, and she smiled. "Jim Woodward, you're a terrible tease at the best and worst of times. I'm doing well. Come in." She held out her hand. When Jim took it, Laura felt how different his grip was than Morgan's powerful, yet gentle one.

Jim put his hat on the edge of Laura's desk and took the chair next to hers. He searched her features. "Is it true? That you were temporarily blinded? All I see is a nasty cut on the temple and a few scratches on your cheek."

Laura squeezed Jim's hand, then released it. "Put the emphasis on *temporarily*, Jim. The doctor says two weeks at the most in this situation, and I'll be good as new."

Morgan sat down on a chair next to Laura's. She was putting on a sunny smile and brave act for the officer. At least she didn't put on an act for Morgan. But he didn't like the intimacy Woodward had established with her. Was there something between them, despite her earlier protests? Jealousy, an emotion he'd rarely felt before, became screamingly alive within him.

"Actually," Laura went on, "Morgan has been a godsend for me. I saved him from getting struck by that limo at the airport, but he's saved me from a lot of days without help around here."

"Morgan?" Jim Woodward lifted his eyes, looking at him for a long time.

Laura frowned, hearing a question in Jim's voice. "Yes, Morgan Ramsey. I thought you'd introduce yourselves at the door."

Uncomfortable beneath Woodward's sudden scrutiny, Morgan tinkered with the tape in the cassette recorder. "We did, Laura," he managed without reaction. "Are you ready to get this interview underway?"

"Sure. Jim, you set?"

The marine corps officer frowned, reluctantly returning his attention to Laura. "Of course."

Lighting-quick tension shot through the office and it confused Laura. Why was Jim suddenly stiff and formal? And Morgan was acting oddly, too. If only she could see! Had they taken an immediate dislike to each other, after all? Unable to sort out the reasons, Laura had to settle for starting the interview.

With the interview completed, Morgan left the office. For nearly an hour, Woodward had stared hard at him, as if fixing a memory in the back of his mind. Dammit! He went to the kitchen and poured himself a cup of coffee. His face was somewhat altered since 1970, but a mustache wasn't much of a disguise. He broke out in a cold sweat. What if Woodward mentioned his suspicions to Laura? What if he went to the press?

"Laura, do you know anything about this Morgan Ramsey?" Jim asked confidentially.

She smiled. "He's an American who works overseas in France. Why, Jim?"

The officer shook his head. "I don't know. The man looks familiar, but I can't place his face. I could swear I know him."

Laughing lightly, Laura murmured, "With your photographic memory, Jim, I'm sure you'll come up with the answer."

"He was uncomfortable with me being here. You couldn't notice it, but I did."

"I don't think Morgan is used to sitting still in an office for an hour, taping an interview," she returned blithely. "He's strictly the outdoors type."

"Maybe," Jim conceded, getting to his feet. "How'd he get that scar?"

"In Vietnam."

"Oh."

"Yes, he was a captain in the marine corps during the conflict. Why?"

Shaking his head, Jim muttered, "There's something I don't trust about him, Laura. Are you sure you're safe with him here? You live alone—"

"Jim, no one's more trustworthy than Morgan Ramsey. Remember, I've been on the receiving end of his care since the accident." Laura got to her feet.

Undaunted, Jim placed his hand beneath her elbow to lead her from the room. "Maybe," he said. As he guided her to the front door, he lowered his voice. "Look, if you need help, call me. You have my office and home numbers."

Warmed by his protectiveness, Laura placed a hand on his arm. "Thanks, Jim, but everything's fine."

"Who does he work for over in France? Will you find out for me? I want to run a check on that guy. He looks suspicious."

Stopping at the door, Laura grimaced. "Jim, you're overreacting."

"Do you know who he works for?"

Hesitating, Laura bit down on her lower lip. "Well . . . no, I don't. I assumed it was for an American company."

"Check it out for me, will you, tiger?"

"Jim—"

"Please, Laura? Do me this favor?"

Favors were the name of the game at the Pentagon, Laura knew from many years of working with the brass there. They were called blue chips. If a chip was tossed in her direction, she had to reciprocate when the chip was called in by the person who had originally granted the favor. Well, Jim had granted this interview, and now she owed him. If she wanted more cooperation from him in the future, she'd have to acquiesce to his request. "All right, Jim, I'll find out."

"And you'll call me right away?"

Upset he was pressing so hard, she muttered. "Yes, I'll call you right away."

Chapter Five

"What's wrong? You look worried." Morgan roused himself from where he was leaning against the drainboard, a cup of coffee in hand.

Laura stood at the entrance to the kitchen. "I do?"

He smiled slightly and walked over, leading her to the chair to sit down. "You never could hide anything with that face of yours."

"Oh."

"That's not a sin. Coffee?"

"No, I'd rather have a glass of orange juice."

Morgan set his cup down on the table and crossed to the refrigerator. "I noticed you and the captain were on pretty friendly terms with each other." He poured the juice into a glass.

She laughed softly. "Morgan Ramsey, are you jealous?"

Disgruntled, he placed the glass in front of her, then sat down at her elbow. "I guess I am."

Reaching over, she found his arm, allowing her fingers to rest on it. "There's nothing to be jealous of. Jim Woodward is a resource for me when I want to write on a topic involving the marine corps. He's their public relations officer at the Pentagon."

Morgan felt his stomach start to knot. Great. That guy would be in a position to have access to more information than most. Had he recognized him? Sweat popped out on his brow. Tearing himself from his fear of being recognized, he gazed over at Laura's serene features. She appeared untouched in a world that had the capability of slashing someone's life apart in seconds.

"So why did you appear upset earlier? Did he say something to you?"

She took a swallow of the juice. "He thinks he knows you, Morgan, but he can't place from where. He asked a favor of me." The unhappiness came out in her voice and she didn't try to disguise it. "Sometimes he gets overly protective of me—just like a big brother."

Morgan held the cup very still between his hands. "What did he want from you?"

"He asked me to find out what company you work for over in France. I told him I thought it was an American one, but wasn't sure." She gripped his arm more tightly. "I'm sorry, Morgan."

He captured her cool, damp fingers by placing his hand on top of hers. "Don't be. That's all he wanted to know?"

"Yes, just the name of your employer. I guess he's going to run a check on you."

Fear cascaded through him. "Isn't he jumping to conclusions? Or is he always this dramatic about another man being in your life?"

Her lips quirked. "I know it's none of his business. He shouldn't be nosing around like this. I'm disappointed in him. I don't know why he's doing it."

"Maybe the guy likes you a lot more than you realized, and he's threatened by the fact that I'm here twenty-four hours a day."

Laura was going to deny Morgan's statement at first, but his reasoning was logical. Jim did ask her out on a date every once in a while, although she always declined. "Oh, dear. Why am I so naive sometimes?"

"Because you see only the best qualities in all of us, Laura," he said quietly. "You're not capable of seeing our worst side—our devious or selfish or greedy side."

His voice was like a balm over her heart, and Laura managed a strangled laugh. "Guilty as charged. Oh, why didn't I realize that Jim's probably jealous?"

"It's a small thing," Morgan said, wrestling with his own fears.

"Tell me where you work so I can rectify this situation in a hurry."

Morgan tightened his hand over hers. "I'm a captain in the French Foreign Legion, Laura. I've been there for the past six years. In a few months I can re-enlist, if I want."

"Oh, dear." The French Foreign Legion! Laura knew a great deal about that particular branch of military service. She'd done a long, thorough article on it for a major national magazine a year ago.

Morgan saw the surprise, then confusion in her widening blue eyes. "When Woodward runs a check on me, he's going to find a dead end," he promised. "The Legion never divulges much of anything about the men who serve her."

Laura's mind spun with questions and no answers. "You're right, the Legion keeps every man's identity and record classified." And men from all over the world joined the Legion to escape old ways of life, to make new ones for themselves. "Morgan, why did you join?"

"Is this between you and me, or does this include Woodward?"

"No, just me."

Believing her, Morgan said, "After I recovered from my wounds, I didn't want to come stateside. I'm a good soldier, Laura, and I felt I'd be of use in the Legion." That wasn't a total lie, but it was far from the entire truth. He watched the expression on her face closely. There was compassion in Laura's eyes, and the way the corners of her mouth pulled in, he knew she felt deeply for him. "It wasn't so bad, little swan."

"But, the Legion is so hard on its men! I mean, they're considered the best of the mercenaries."

"Hard, yes. But not cruel."

"And you build bridges for them?"

"Yes, I have a degree in engineering. I build bridges, dig ditches and help clear land for airport runways in some of the most godforsaken spots on this earth. Sometimes we provide protection or perform other military duties."

"But what about your family? It must be terribly hard on them for you to be overseas like that."

He hung his head, real anguish serrating him. "Yeah, it's rough on them," he admitted thickly.

It was on the tip of her tongue to delve further into his past, but Laura sensed the time was not right. Something terrible had happened to his company in Vietnam. That much she was sure of. And whatever it was, Morgan still carried guilt or grief because of it. Had he gone to the Legion to escape his past? So many men did just that. Perhaps over the next week he would share his reasons with her.

Trying to buoy the sudden despair she heard in his voice, Laura found his hand and gripped it. "I don't know about you, but I'm starved. If you want, we could go to a restaurant and treat ourselves. We've both been housebound, and I can sense that you're restless."

Morgan smiled, wanting to lean forward the press her ripe lips against his mouth. She was still awkward with her blindness, and to go out in public would be exhausting for her. She'd forsaken her own welfare in order to help him. "No, let's stay here. I'll make us lunch, and then I'll get to work typing up that interview with Woodward. Maybe by tonight you and I can get it into some kind of article form.''

Laura murmured his name and slid her arms around him. Resting her head against his jaw, she whispered, ''You're so special, Morgan.''

He embraced her for a long moment, relishing her warmth and softness against him. The fragrance of orange blossoms encircled him, and he inhaled the scent deeply. ''Come on, Ms. Bennett, let's get this dog-and-pony show on the road. We've got work to do this afternoon.''

Just being in his arms made her feel safe and loved. She nestled her head against Morgan's shoulder, content as never before. ''I'll be so glad when I get my sight back, Morgan. So glad....''

''You'd think that after seven days I'd at least be able to see some light, Morgan.'' Laura touched the healing cut on her temple as she sat down on the rug in front of the fireplace.

''Dr. Taggert just checked you yesterday, Laura. He said the swelling's going down, but it hasn't disappeared yet. Give it another week, my impatient swan. Here's your popcorn.'' Morgan brought over a bowl of freshly popped corn and placed it in her lap. She looked fetching in her white cotton gown and lavender robe as she sat in front of the fire. He liked their nightly custom of sitting on the floor, talking, eating popcorn and feeling the warmth of the fire after working all day.

"Thanks." Laura picked disinterestedly at the popcorn. She felt Morgan lie down nearby, always within an arm's distance from her. "I'm just getting panicky, Morgan. What if I don't see?"

He reached over, catching her hand in midair. "You will. I've got a gut feeling on this, Laura. Just hang in there. You're worrying too much, and you aren't sleeping at night the way you should."

She laughed abruptly. "Like last night? I sat up screaming during a nightmare, and you almost killed yourself getting to my room.'

"I thought someone had broken into the house and was attacking you," Morgan said gently. The right toe of his foot still ached from where he'd stubbed it as he ran down the hall to her room.

"Still," Laura murmured, "you hurt yourself." She had fallen into his arms, wildly aware of his rock-hard chest beneath her cheek as he'd embraced her. For the next ten minutes, Morgan had held and rocked her as she cried. They were tears of fear—fear of never being able to see again. His strength was now her strength.

Placing the bowl on the carpeted floor, Laura stretched out on her stomach, her hands beneath her cheek as she faced him. The silence settled soothingly around them. "Morgan?"

He watched her eyes beneath the thick gold lashes that framed them. If Laura only knew how beautiful she was, or how desirable.... "Yes?" The word stuck in his throat, his heart beginning a slow, sledgehammer pound.

"Tell me about your family. What's Aly like?"

Laura was like an elegant swan, lying prone on the carpet, her face shadowed and thoughtful. Morgan rolled onto his side, only inches away from her. "Spunky," he said, a faraway tone in his voice. "Red haired, tenacious and bold."

"And Noah? Is he older or younger than you?"

Morgan reached out, taming several strands of her blond hair away from her flushed cheek, placing them behind her small ear. "Three years younger. He's the better-looking of the two of us."

Laura smiled, closing her eyes. "That's *your* opinion, Morgan. How would you describe Noah?"

He laid his head down on his arms and stared across at her. There had been tenderness in her voice. "Reliable. And not as hard or driven as I am."

"What drives you, Morgan?"

He sighed. "My dad, I guess. He had thirty years in the air force and came out a general. All his life he expected the three of us to go into the service of our choice. With his illustrious career as an example, I wanted to be exactly like him. You'd have to meet him to understand what I'm saying. He didn't brainwash any of us into going into the military. It was just his presence, his belief in defending this country and the fact that each one of us could make a difference that inspired me, I guess."

Laura heard the wistfulness in Morgan's voice. "How did your parents meet?"

"Mom was a nurse over in Korea during the war. Her MASH unit got overrun by the Communists, and the entire staff was taken prisoner. She escaped from the prison about fifty miles north of the demilitarized zone and was in the process of trying to make her way back to South Korea. Dad was flying his plane over the north when he was jumped by six MIGS and was shot down. He bailed out and my mother followed the parachute to where he landed. They teamed up and spent the next week dodging the Communists trying to recapture them.''

Laura rested her head against her hand. "What an exciting way to meet."

"It was pure hell," Morgan said. "Dad was wounded, and Mom ended up being the one who got them back to safe territory."

"And they fell in love during their escape?"

Morgan smiled, watching the sudden animation in Laura's eyes. "Yes, they did. I guess they fought like cats and dogs. Dad can be a bulldog sometimes—a family trait he passed on to all of us, I'm afraid." Morgan chuckled. "He was delirious and swore that south was a certain direction. Mom knew it wasn't. She said they got into a lot of shouting matches on that trip out of enemy territory."

"Sounds like the three of you children inherited the best from both of them," Laura whispered. "You have your father's tenacity and your mother's sensitivity."

Rolling over on his back, Morgan tucked his hands behind his head and stared up at the ceiling. An ache to see his family once again overwhelmed him. "If you met my family," he said thickly, "you'd love them.

They're all individuals, but each one is caring and responsible.''

Laura reached out, her hand coming in contact with his chest. She felt his heart beating hard beneath her palm. "Have you told them you're here in the States yet?"

Her hand eased the ache in his heart. Morgan turned, looking up into her features. "No—" Her eyes were shadowed with pain—his pain. "It wouldn't be wise" was all he could say.

"Oh, Morgan, are you sure?" Laura moved into a sitting position, resting her hands in her lap.

"Very," he growled, rising to his feet. "I'm getting tired, Laura. How about you?"

Swallowing against the lump in her throat, Laura got up with his help. Morgan's shields were back in place. She'd pushed too far into his past. "It's supposed to be sunny and sixty-five degrees tomorrow. I'd like to plant my begonias. Would you help me?"

Her face was guileless, Morgan thought as he stood next to her, his hand gripping hers. "Yeah, planting something sounds positive," he agreed.

The phone on her bedroom nightstand awoke Laura the next morning. Unable to check the time, she groped for and found the receiver.

"Hello?" she said, her voice husky with sleep.

"Laura? It's Jim Woodward. I'm sorry, did I wake you?"

Sitting up, she rubbed her eyes. "Uh, that's all right, Jim. What time is it?"

"Nearly nine. Look, I'm sorry to disturb you, but I think you should know something about this guy Morgan Ramsey."

Pushing the hair away from her eyes, Laura asked, "What?"

"I traced his name through our computers, and there was no Morgan Ramsey in the marine corps during the Vietnam conflict. I know that face, Laura. Right now I'm searching through our photographic files in my spare time. This bothers me. Men don't go into the Foreign Legion unless they want to escape the past. I'm positive Ramsey isn't his real name."

Upset, Laura said, "Look, Jim, I believe him. I *know* Morgan was in Vietnam."

Woodward laughed tightly. "Then it was under another name. I'm sending this info to the CIA. Maybe they can get a handle on him."

"Jim, this isn't necessary!" Her voice had risen, and Laura suddenly realized that Morgan might be able to hear her. She didn't know if the door to her bedroom was open or closed.

"But it is."

"He's not a convict, Jim!"

"Look, I didn't mean to upset you, Laura. It's just that this guy is hiding something. I don't like the fact that he's there with you all the time."

She gripped the phone. "That's really the reason, isn't it, Jim?"

"What?"

"Don't play games with me. I think you're being protective. I don't understand why you're doing this, Jim."

"I've liked you for a long time, Laura—you know that."

Keeping the anger from her voice, she pleaded with him, "Jim, leave Morgan's past alone. Please. He's not a threat to me in any way. The man is simply trying to repay me for saving his life. That's all."

Jim's voice grew dark. "Not from what I could see. You're blind right now, Laura. You don't see how he looks at you. It's as if he's staked his claim, and I don't like it."

"Jim, you're way out of line. My private life is my own, not yours. And he's certainly hasn't 'staked a claim' on me. How can you be so distrusting when the man hasn't done anything to deserve it?"

"Laura, you're angry, and I didn't mean to make you feel that way."

"You're darned right I am. What if someone started snooping into your past?"

"I don't have anything to hide," Jim said tightly. "When I get anything more on him, I'll call you."

Her voice shook with anger. "No, Jim, don't call. You're invading my privacy. You see, I trust Morgan. I don't *care* what his past is. I judge people on how they treat me, not by their names, their pasts or whatever else. Goodbye!" She groped until she found the phone cradle, then dropped the receiver into it. The day wasn't starting off on the right foot at all. Jim

Woodward was jealous and protective of her in a way she'd never fathom.

"Men and their games!" she grumped, throwing off the covers. As she placed her feet on the floor, she gasped. The world was no longer black in front of her eyes. It was a dark gray, instead. She placed her hand in front of her face; she could barely make out the outline of it.

She sat for several minutes, assimilating her discovery. Her vision was returning! She was able to discern shadow from light. If she held something close to her eyes, placing it in the sunlight cascading through the ruffled pink curtains, she could make out its general shape, but not the color. Tears streamed from her eyes and ran down her cheeks. She was going to see again! *Oh, God, thank you!*

But her happiness eroded as Jim's phone call came back to haunt her. She sat on the edge of the bed, scuffing her toe into the carpet. She couldn't believe Morgan was lying to her about his family or Vietnam because of the emotion in his voice when he spoke about them.

After getting her morning bath and washing her hair, she put on the clothes Morgan had laid out for her to wear the night before. Troubled, she made her way to the kitchen. She stopped at the entrance, narrowing her eyes, straining to discover if she could see anything. Something moved near the counter—a dark shape against the sunlight pouring in through the windows.

"Morgan?"

Morgan turned, still immersed in thought. "Good morning." Laura looked pretty in the lavender dolman-sleeved blouse and threadbare jeans. Today she wanted to plant begonias and had asked for her worst clothes to wear. Somehow, Morgan thought, feeling his heart squeeze with fresh feelings of happiness, she looked pretty despite her disheveled clothes. Her smile was uncertain, and he noticed she was pale.

"That phone call woke you, didn't it?" he asked, walking over and leading her to the chair at the table.

"Yes."

"Woodward?" he guessed, putting slices of bread into the toaster.

She heard the edge to his tone. "How did you know?"

"A gut feeling." Bad news always traveled fast. "What did he have to say?"

If only she could see the expression on Morgan's face! It would tell her so much. Laura chewed on her lower lip. "Not much. Just that he swore he recognized you and was now going through photo files at the Pentagon to see if he could find something on you."

Morgan's hands froze over the toast he was buttering. According to what he could find out last year when his full memory had returned, there had been plenty of press and photos on the loss of his men on Hill 164. Sooner or later Jim Woodward would stumble onto the truth. He set the toast aside and divided the scrambled eggs between the two plates. Bringing them over to the table, he set them down.

"Let it pass, Laura. Woodward is chasing up blind alleys for no reason. Come on, let's eat a hearty breakfast and get to planting those begonia bulbs."

Laura hesitated. Should she tell Morgan that her sight was returning? And that she knew Ramsey wasn't his last name? She sensed his nervousness. Something told her that he'd disappear if she admitted either thing. Picking up the fork, she forced herself to eat. The last thing she wanted was for him to walk out of her life.

"Laura?" Morgan reached over, sliding his hand along her shoulder. "What's wrong?"

Just the concerned tenor of his voice unstrung her. Tears welled up in her eyes and she quickly shut them. Morgan must not know how much he'd come to mean to her in such a short time. "N-nothing."

"It's Woodward's phone call that's bothering you, isn't it?"

She put her fork down on her plate. "Yes."

Morgan sat very still. If he told her the truth, she'd want him out of her life. And that shook him like nothing else had in the past year. He absorbed her concerned features. How could someone so small and delicate have captured his heart so thoroughly in one week's time? Suddenly the thought of losing Laura was almost too much to bear.

Miserably Morgan moved the plates aside. He moved his chair next to Laura's and took her hands. "We have to talk," he whispered hoarsely.

Laura gripped his hands. They were cold, almost icy. Morgan's face was heavily lined, and his gray eyes were desolate-looking as he held her gaze. She stilled her joy over her steadily improving eyesight. Morgan's plight was far more important to her heart. "Tell me," she urged softly.

"You won't want me to stay after I tell you, Laura," he warned.

She shook her head, tightening her hands on his. "Let me be the judge of that, Morgan. What happened in your past that still haunts you?"

Taking a deep breath, he let the pain-filled words flow from his conscience and heart. "In January of 1970 I was commanding a company of marines in the I Corps area of Vietnam. My assistant company commander, Lieutenant Stephen Cantrell, was my best friend. Both of us questioned the orders to put our company on Hill 164, which was deep within enemy territory. When I called Colonel Jack Armstrong, he told me the tactical plan had been approved by his superiors, right up the line. He promised we'd have air and artillery support just in case the NVA got aggressive and started testing our defenses."

Morgan shut his eyes, reliving the nightmare. "We were up on that lousy hill for two days, getting the hell rocketed out of us. I was losing men fast. A lot of the time we couldn't even get medevac in to take out the wounded, because the NVA had us pinned down. Every time I requested permission to withdraw, Armstrong insisted we stay." His voice grew husky. "And then they hit us with at least a battalion of NVA. We fought all night. I called for air and artillery, but they weren't available. By dawn there were fifteen of us left. Then came the final attack. It was hand-to-hand combat. The last thing I remember was Stephen getting shot and falling beside me. I saw an NVA officer charge me with his bayonet.'' He pointed to the scar on his face. ''I remember getting cut. And then I blanked out.''

''My God,'' Laura said, her voice quavering, ''I remember now . . . you're Captain Morgan Trayhern.''

He studied her in silence, watching the myriad emotions play across her face. Morgan expected her to withdraw her hands from his. ''Yeah, that's me.''

Tears stung Laura's eyes, and she sniffed. ''But the press and Pentagon accused you of being a traitor, of leaving your post before your men died.'' She lifted her hand, sliding it across his shoulder, seeing his eyes bleak with pain. ''I can't believe you ran, not after the way you've taken care of me. Morgan, you aren't capable of that.''

A corner of his mouth lifted and he glanced over at her. ''I didn't run, Laura. It was all a fabrication.''

''How?''

He bowed his head, and his words were harsh. ''Twenty-four hours later, according to Colonel Armstrong, they managed to get a relief column to Hill 164. They found two of us alive—me and Private Lenny Miles. The doctors sent me to Japan, to a hospital controlled by the CIA. The surgeons told Armstrong I was going to die. I had a fractured skull and two bayonet wounds in my chest.

Laura cringed. ''Oh, Morgan . . .''

"That isn't the worst of it," he growled. "After all the surgery and a week in a coma, I survived. Armstrong flew over to Japan and paid me a visit. When I became conscious, I found I'd lost my memory. I didn't know who I was, where I was or anything else. Because of the damage to my brain, the doctors felt I'd never regain my memory or my sense of smell. Armstrong knew it and fabricated a new identity and personal history for me. My name was Morgan Ramsey and I was a CIA operative. I had been wounded in Laos on assignment and was in Japan to recuperate. He said that my next assignment would be to join the French Foreign Legion and act as a mole in that outfit, giving the CIA information as they needed it. Before Armstrong left, he gave me a file covering my life history. I didn't know any differently, so I swallowed my 'past,' never dreaming I'd been lied to."

Horror engulfed Laura, and she placed a hand across her mouth. Morgan's face mirrored his anguish. "What they've done is illegal," she whispered angrily. "They've framed you! Your name and face were splashed across every major television network and newspaper for at least a month. Your poor family..."

"Yeah, they've suffered more than anyone," Morgan ground out. "A year ago I was climbing a cliff face with my company when the rope broke. I fell thirty feet to the ground and struck my head. Luckily I had a helmet on, or I'm sure it would have split open my skull," he said ruefully. "But what the accident did was slowly start to bring my memory back. I'd been seeing the faces of certain people in my dreams for the six previous years, and never knew who they were. Now I knew. They were my parents, my brother, Noah, and my sister, Aly.''

"And did you contact General Armstrong once you knew the truth?"

"I did. The CIA operative I'd been working with in Marseilles from time to time suddenly disappeared. I called the Pentagon to talk with General Kip Young, who had been my battalion commander back in 1970, but no one would talk to me." Morgan got up and paced the kitchen. "For the rest of the year, I wondered what the hell to do. I knew from what little I'd investigated about myself that I'd been branded the consummate traitor to this country. And then two weeks ago I got a phone call from the commandant of the Legion. He ordered me to fly to D.C., and wouldn't say why. Of course I had to follow orders. When I got stateside, I found out that Armstrong was dying. He wanted to see me to tell me that sometimes one good man had to be sacrificed for a dedicated group of military officers."

Her heart squeezed with anguish at the hardness and tension in Morgan's face. "Was Armstrong going to clear you?"

"Hell, no!" Morgan exploded, halting in the center of the kitchen. "The bastard just wanted to get things off his chest and make everything right with his Maker. Young warned me that if I tried to stay in D.C. or expose the snafu I wouldn't get anywhere." He ran his fingers through his hair. "I wanted to see my family, but I knew that under the circumstances it was impossible. They've gone through enough pain and hardship for my sake. When you saw me at the airport that morning, I was tied in knots. That's why I stepped in front of that limo without looking. I wasn't thinking straight. I was all wrapped up in my emotions.''

Laura sat there, the shock and silence settling over her. Her mind spun with questions and possible answers. She saw him staring at her, doubt in his eyes. ''I believe you, Morgan,'' she hurried to assure him.

The words fell softly against his throttled anger and fear. The three words offered him hope for once, instead of despair. Laura looked diminutive sitting there, her hands tense in her lap as she gazed up in his direction. ''Besides my family, you're the only other person who ever would,'' Morgan responded bitterly.

Laura got to her feet and walked slowly in his direction, pretending she was still blind by holding out her hand. She lifted her arms once she made contact with Morgan, placing them around his sagging shoulders. There was incredible tension in him as she pressed herself against him. ''You're the bravest man I've ever met,'' she whispered against his ear. ''And you're so tired. . . .''

Just Laura's sweet contact broke Morgan. With a groan he swept his arms around her, nearly crushing her. He buried his face in her hair, a sob trying to wrench from deep within him. But he held it back as he always did. He felt her belief in him shatter all his bitterness.

"Just let me hold you," Laura crooned, beginning to stroke his short, black hair with her trembling fingers.

Morgan's world spun around Laura, the strength of her slight form against him giving him sustenance, when he'd had so little the past seven years. He felt her slender arms holding him more firmly, offering solace. The pain in his heart was transformed, and a ragged sigh broke from the tortured line of his mouth.

"You're so damn giving," Morgan rasped, pressing a kiss to her hair. "I couldn't believe you'd stepped out in front of that limo for me. It just exploded my world." He nuzzled into the thick strands of her hair. "You're so small and yet so strong. Strong in ways I'm not, Laura...."

His mouth hungrily trailed a path of fire from her temple to her cheek. "Morgan," she breathed, lifting her lips to his assault, and felt his mouth claim hers with fiery urgency, drinking her into his soul. Surrendering to him, she relaxed within his powerful grip, spiraling into a cauldron of simmering desire. Eagerly she returned his kiss, matching his hunger with her own. He was at once demanding, claiming her, stealing her breath—her heart—as his sweet assault continued. Her senses reeled until her limbs felt weak beneath his onslaught.

Tearing his mouth from hers, Morgan staggered back a step, surprised at his own ferocity and need. Laura swayed uncertainly in his arms, and he gripped her, staring down at her sultry blue eyes, flecked with fire. Her lips were pouty from the strength of his kiss, glistening and wanton in the aftermath. And when her lashes slowly lifted and her eyes met his, it was her soft smile that reached his heavily walled heart.

Laura held his unsure gaze, his gray eyes narrowed and stormy. She cradled his face between her hands. "Don't say you're sorry, because I'm not," she murmured unsteadily. "This has been coming ever since we met...."

Morgan stared at her. "And you're not sorry it happened," he said wryly.

"No. No regrets, Morgan." Making a supreme effort, she locked her knees so that she could stand upright. His kiss had shaken her deeply. Allowing her hands to leave his face, she gripped his upper arms. "But right now, more important things have to be addressed."

With her hair mussed she looked wanton. Morgan got a grip on himself. The kiss had been explosive, melding them to each other. "There's not much else left to be addressed," he told her thickly.

Her eyes blazed with indignation. "Oh, yes, there is, Morgan." She pulled out of his arms, noting the surprise on his face at her throaty response. "Come on, let's sit down and talk."

Chapter Six

Y ou know that Armstrong and his cronies framed you. So what are you going to do about it?'' Laura asked. She sat down at the table, watching Morgan's face closely. Her heart squeezed with fresh pain as she saw tears in his eyes for just a moment before he forced them away.

Sasha whined and came over, resting her massive head in Laura's lap, as if to give her comfort. Absently she patted the dog.

''Morgan?''

He sat down heavily. ''I wasn't going to do anything.''

''You mean you were just going to disappear back to France after I got my sight back?'' The idea of

Morgan leaving her was unbearable. They were so close in so many ways—even if their bond was only a week old. Laura reached out and gripped his hand.

"I wasn't going anywhere until I was sure you had your sight back," he muttered, his voice low with feeling.

"Out of duty to me?" Laura guessed.

"At first it was. But getting to know you, I've stayed because I care about you, Laura. I'll never regret that decision," he said, giving her a sad smile.

"And if my sight returns, you'll leave?" She held her breath, wanting him to say no. Wanting him to recognize that there was something good and positive between them as a man and woman that transcended duty.

Morgan looked up at the ceiling, trying to hold together his unraveling emotions. "I—" With a shake of his head he confessed, "I'm not sure what I was going to do, Laura."

She leaned forward, sliding her hand into his. "Why?"

Her voice reminded him of a whisper of breeze through a meadow in summertime. "I know it hasn't been long, but there's something between us, something that's been missing in my life for as long as I can remember." He studied her long, slender fingers, wondering what it would be like to love her. "Maybe I'm tired of running and hiding. I don't know. Being here with you has made me want to stay and explore what we have." He scowled. "Or haven't had...." A self-deprecating smile cut across his mouth. "My dreamer side wants to stay. My logic tells me that as soon as you can see, I should get the hell out of here and go back to France."

Touched, Laura fought her own reactions. If Morgan saw the tears that wanted to spill from her eyes, he might misinterpret them. Gripping his hand, she murmured, "With or without my sight back, Morgan, I want you to stay."

His eyebrows moving up, Morgan studied her parted lips—lips that had yielded so willingly to him earlier. "Why?"

"My first reaction is unselfish. You were framed by Armstrong and Young. If I were in your shoes, I'd fight back. No one has the right to keep you from your family and cheat you of so much that's rightfully yours." She lowered her voice. "My second reason is selfish. I—I want you to stay. We do have something special between us, and I think we deserve the chance to find out what it is."

The sunlight spilled across the table, highlighting her mussed blond hair. Morgan saw the fire blazing in her wide azure eyes, the stubborn set of her chin and the thinning of those full lips. He gently traced her fingers. "You're a scrappy little thing for being as small as you are," he teased roughly. "And you've got a hell of a lot more backbone than I do, Laura."

"Backbone? Oh, God, Morgan, you've endured seven years of hell! That's real strength."

"There's no way to prove my innocence with the American people, Laura. Young will block me at every turn. It's my word against the Pentagon's if I go public.'' He shook his head. ''Think what it would do to my family if I suddenly reappeared. I can do nothing but continue to make them suffer because I can't prove my innocence.''

Anger worked its way through Laura, and she released his hand and stood. ''Morgan Trayhern, you're talking like a loser now! How can you forsake your family and your country and slink back to France because of Young?''

She looked like a vengeful Valkyrie without armor. ''Calm down, Laura. The reality of the situation is that I don't have any other recourse.''

''Yes, you do, Morgan!'' She stamped her foot. ''I don't believe this! As close as you seem to be to your family, you're willing to forsake them without a fight!''

''The odds aren't good,'' Morgan parried. ''If I walk back into my family's life, the reporters will get wind of it.''

''So what? It's just another battle, Morgan. And God knows, you've already been through some battles where you should have died. You didn't.''

Morgan got up and walked over to her, bringing her against him. At first Laura resisted, and then, as he kissed her hair, she yielded to him. ''My little warrioress,'' he teased, inhaling her fragrance, absorbing her strength.

''Morgan, I'm not Don Quixote tilting at windmills,'' she warned tightly. Pushing away far enough to look up at him, Laura held his warm gaze, which was filled with longing. The urge to reach up on tiptoe and kiss away the anguish in his compressed mouth nearly unstrung her. "You forget one thing. I'm an archives expert. I've spent years in the Pentagon file system. Maybe I can discover some unclassified documents, or at least get hold of someone who can help us."

Leaning down, Morgan kissed the tip of her nose. "No one in the military is going to help us, Laura. It would cost him his next rank, or politically sandbag him so he'd have to retire." He shook his head. "No, you won't get any help."

"Damn you!" Laura grated, gripping his upper arms. "Fight back! Fight for what's rightfully yours!"

Stunned by her cry, Morgan stood in the ebbing silence, staring at her. Her eyes were filled with tears. He saw them streak down her flushed cheeks.

"If you're really a Trayhern, you'll fight back," she whispered harshly. "Look at what your mother and father did to escape from North Korea. Did they sit down and cry because they were behind the lines? Did they give up because they were fifty miles from safety? No. And you have the gall to stand here and tell me there's no hope for you, Morgan!" Laura wrenched out of his arms and took several steps away from him.

Smarting beneath her attack, Morgan stalked to the counter and leaned heavily against it. He glared out the window at the carefully kept garden in the backyard. "Dammit, Laura, you're refusing to see how *much* is stacked against me!"

Her breath was rapid and shallow. "Only a coward would run from this," Laura shot back.

Morgan spun around, his hands clenched. Eyes blazing, he advanced on her. "Coward?" he snarled into her face.

She held her ground, glaring back at him. "Yes, a *coward*!" she shouted.

"I ought to—"

"What? Strangle me?" Laura laughed sharply and jabbed him in the chest with her finger. "You're running, Morgan. You're admitting defeat before the battle is ever mounted and fought. You've made all the decisions for your mother and father," she stormed. "And for Noah and Aly." With an angry swipe of her hand, she dried the tears from her face. "And you're making a decision for me, too! What if I want you to stay because I happen to like you? How dare you presume to make those decisions for us!"

Morgan blinked once, watching her turn and stalk off to the living room. The air crackled with her anger and hurt. Rubbing his jaw, burning beneath her salvos, he glared down at the carpet. What a little fighter she was. But a beautiful one. Cursing, he, too, stalked out of the kitchen.

Laura stood by the drapes, looking out the window. Her eyesight had returned completely during the heat of their argument. She teetered between the joy of seeing color and shape clearly once again and the anguish she felt for Morgan. The day was sunny and bright—everything she wasn't right now. Torn between sharing her happy news with Morgan and remaining focused on their immediate problem, Laura dragged in a deep breath of air. Hearing him enter, she jerked her head in his direction. All her joy and desire to confide her happiness in him was smashed. She saw the agony in the slash of his mouth. Her anger evaporated as he walked over to where she stood. There was confusion in his features, and she yearned to reach out and comfort him, but she stood woodenly.

"Has anyone ever accused you of being a first-class hellion?" he demanded.

Lowering her gaze, Laura managed a strained laugh. "Yes. My parents."

Morgan closed his eyes, trying to sort through his feelings. "I don't know, Laura," he whispered. "You crashed into my life, and everything's been topsy-turvy ever since. I didn't mean to seem to be making decisions for you and everyone else."

Laura stopped herself from moving into his arms. "Why don't you let your family decide if they want to enter the fray, Morgan?" She lifted her eyes to his. "And why don't you ask me if I'm willing to help you in your fight to get back your good name?"

Morgan held her tear-filled eyes—blue eyes that were lustrous and gentle with understanding. "I-it's been a long time since someone was on my side, Laura."

"I know." She reached out, finding his hand, holding it. "All you've known since 1970 has been loneliness and the burden of carrying all those memories by yourself. You don't have to now. I'm sure your family would rather see you and help support you in this fight than see you leave for France."

He glanced at her. "You're my biggest fan."

"I've been on the receiving end of your care, remember?" Her voice was hoarse with suppressed sobs. "Morgan, you've proved yourself to me by your actions. It's easy for me to stand here and tell you that I'll help you with every particle of my being. I believe in you."

Lifting Laura's hand, Morgan pressed a kiss to the back of it. Her flesh was firm and warm beneath his mouth. "Okay, little swan, you've convinced me I should try."

Laura moved in front of him. "You've got to stay for yourself, Morgan, not because I want it."

"I understand."

She took a deep breath. "I'm going to test you on that right now."

"What do you mean?" He saw her eyes fraught with fear, not understanding her challenge.

"This morning when I got up, I could see again, Morgan. I've got my sight back."

Stunned, he stared at her for a long moment. Then he grinned. "Wonderful!" he murmured, crushing her against him.

Wanting to share his elation but still uncertain of the consequences of her admission, she allowed him to release her. Relief was etched in his eyes as he cupped her face, staring deeply into hers.

"You can see," he said, his voice quavering.

"Y-yes."

"God, that's good news," Morgan said fervently. If he hadn't been mired in his own self-pity earlier, he thought, he would have noted the dancing highlights in her eyes this morning which hadn't been there before. He sobered suddenly, noticing that Laura wasn't smiling.

"Are you happy?"

She nodded. "Yes, in one way."

"What are you talking about?"

Stepping away from his powerful presence, Laura held his gaze. "I'm no longer blind, Morgan. That frees you of any further obligation to me." She licked her lips. "I don't want you staying here because of what you might owe me. That wouldn't be right. I wanted you to know I can see before you make a final decision on whether you leave for France or stay."

"You've got a lot of courage," he told her.

"I won't lie to you, Morgan. God knows, you've been lied to enough."

He walked over to the couch and sat down. Laura stood at the window, the sunlight caressing her small, proud form. He frowned. "Come here."

Laura came and sat down. Morgan put his arm around her shoulders and drew her to him. Resting her hand against his chest, she could feel the anvil beat of his heart. Weary from the exhilaration and fear of the past half hour, she closed her eyes, resting her head against his shoulder.

"First things first," he told her. "I need to take you to Dr. Taggert and get a clean bill of health on your eyesight."

"I forgot all about that," Laura admitted.

Chuckling softly, Morgan said, "I figured. You're really like the Trayherns in one way—you've got that bulldog tenacity. Once you bite into something, you won't let go of it.''

"You're worth fighting for," Laura murmured, wanting nothing more than to be held.

"Yeah, you've proved that to me." Morgan stared at the fireplace, deep in thought. "If Dr. Taggert says you're fine, I think we should fly down to Florida to visit my parents."

Joy raced through Laura. She lifted her head, drowning in his gray eyes. "Then you're going to stay and fight it out?"

He grinned. "Do I have a choice, little swan?"

She smiled. "Not with me around, you don't."

"You've got my mother's courage—I think my family is going to like you, Laura."

"I already like their elder son. How could I not like them?"

He ran his fingers in an idle pattern on her shoulder and arm. "I don't know which to do—call them or just show up on their doorstep."

"Call them," Laura begged. "Don't shock them by appearing unannounced, Morgan."

She was right. Giving her a hug, he got up. "Come into the kitchen with me. I'll make the call from there."

"Do you still remember their phone number?"

He grinned and grabbed her hand, leading her into the other room. "That phone number haunted me for years before I found out what it meant. After I regained my memory, I knew it was my folks'."

Morgan felt shaky as he picked up the phone and dialed. What would his parents say? What kind of reception would he get? Did they believe he was a traitor? The phone rang three times before it was answered.

"Trayhern residence, Rachel speaking."

Morgan's throat constricted. "Mom? It's Morgan," he rasped unsteadily. "I—I'm calling from Washington, D.C.." The silence seemed to explode with her shock. He heard his mother gasp and utter a small cry.

"Morgan? Morgan, is that really you?"

Tears stung his eyes, and his voice mirrored his emotions. "Yeah, Mom, it's me. Look, I've got a lot of explaining to do, and I don't want to do it over the phone. Can I fly down and see you and Dad?"

"Of course," she sobbed. "Are you all right?"

"Sure, Mom. I'm fine." Morgan glanced over at Laura. She was crying, too. He swallowed hard. "Dad? Is he okay?"

"Fine. Just fine," Rachel assured him. "We didn't know if you were dead or alive. Where have you been? And why haven't you or the Pentagon contacted us?"

"Mom, I'm not a traitor," Morgan whispered, his voice hardening. "Look, I'll answer all your questions once I get there. I'd like to bring a friend of mine along—Laura Bennett. She's important to me . . . and to what's happened of late."

"Of course, bring her with you."

Exhilaration soared through him. "God, it's good to hear your voice, Mom."

"Oh, honey, you'll never know how much your dad and I prayed for you. I'd let you talk to him, but he's at the golf course right now."

"That's okay. And Noah? Aly? How are they?"

Laughing with joy, Rachel said, "Noah's stationed down in Miami. He's married now and has a beautiful daughter and another baby on the way."

Pain jagged through Morgan. "A daughter?" How much had he missed in seven years?

"Yes. He's married the loveliest woman, Morgan. Her name is Kit, and she's so much like Alyssa."

"How is my little sister?" he asked, choking up again at memories of Aly's red hair in pigtails.

"She's been a navy pilot for a year now. Graduated with honors from Annapolis and the Pensacola flight school."

"I'll bet she's having a hell of a good time." Morgan laughed, feeling the weight of years sliding off his shoulders.

"Aly recently married, too, but she's continuing her career for now."

"Good for her. Look, Mom, let me give the number where I'm staying. When Dad gets in, have him call me?"

"Of course, honey."

Morgan repeated Laura's number. He found himself wanting to continue talking, but knew it was wiser to wait until the family had gathered. "Can Noah and his family make it up to see us?"

Laura smiled, warming when he said "us." She walked over and gripped Morgan's hand, giving him a look of pride. Just the satisfaction in his eyes told her everything. It had been the right decision. For all of them.

"I'm going to call him and Aly right now, Morgan."

"Look, Mom, don't tell anyone except the immediate family that I'm alive and stateside. Promise?"

"Well . . . sure."

He knew his mother well enough to know that without his warning against it she'd call every one of their relatives with the news. "Listen, I've got a lot of explaining to do. Right now it wouldn't be wise to let the press or anyone we can't trust get a hold of the fact that I'm back. Okay? Legally I'm still considered a traitor. If the authorities found out I was here, they might toss me in jail and throw away the key."

"I understand, honey," his mother agreed. "As soon as your dad gets in, he'll call you. I know he's going to be so happy. So happy. . . ."

Morgan wanted to cry right along with his mother. He managed a lopsided smile filled with emotion. "We'll make plane reservations right now, Mom. Chances are, by the time Dad calls, we'll be booked on tomorrow's flight."

"I'm so happy you're back, Morgan," Rachel said, weeping. "Hurry home to us. We love you so much."

"I love all of you," Morgan replied brokenly. "Goodbye, Mom."

"Hurry home to us, Morgan. Hurry. . . ."

A deluge of stored emotions and memories swelled through Morgan as he gently replaced the phone back in the cradle. He felt Laura slide her arm around his waist, drawing him into her arms. Holding her for a long time, he finally whispered, "That was my Mom. She was glad to hear from me."

Laughing shakily, Laura hugged him tightly. "Of course she was!"

The heavy walls he'd erected around his heart fell beneath Laura's embrace. With a groan Morgan held her close "You're something else, Laura Bennett . . ." He pressed his mouth to the smooth slope of her cheek, inhaling her flowery fragrance.

Kissing him quickly and stepping away out of fear at the strength of her own emotions, Laura said breathlessly, "Let me call Dr. Taggert and get this examination out of the way. You should stay here and wait for the call from your dad."

Laura's cheeks were flushed and her eyes sparkled with incredible happiness. Morgan quelled his desire to grab her and bring her back into his arms. "No, I'll go with you. Dad will call back if necessary."

She nodded, unable to stop smiling. "I'm so proud of you, Morgan."

Reaching out, Morgan gripped her fingers. "I've never met anyone like you, Laura. So much bravery in such a little package." He grinned. "What do you say we get this show on the road?"

He was achingly boyish in that split second. Laura saw the years of pain and tension fall away from his lined features. For a moment, the breath was stolen from her as she watched his mobile mouth broaden with a genuine smile. His eyes had lightened in color, the shadows in them no longer present. Yearning to reach out, draw him to her and love him, she said huskily, "Yes, let's get this show on the road, Captain Trayhern. We've got dragons to slay."

Laughing, Morgan spanned her small waist, lifting her off her feet. "Sweetheart, I'm no knight in shining armor. More like Don Quixote with you as Sancho Panza at my side." Gently he set her down, sliding his hands across her shoulders, up her neck to her cheeks. "Be my faithful squire?" he asked, studying her darkening blue eyes dancing with gold highlights.

Sobering, Laura nodded, drowning in the silver fire of Morgan's eyes. "Yes, I'll be your partner in this battle. We can't lose, Morgan. We have truth on our side."

He caressed her lips with his, feeling them part beneath his exploration. "You're so sweet and innocent," he breathed against her.

Closing her eyes, Laura molded her lips to his mouth, feeling the texture and strength that was only him. "My belief in you is all I need."

Groaning, Morgan devoured her offering, kissing her hotly. Laura sagged against him, and Morgan felt his world narrowing to only her unshakable belief in him. As he tasted the depths of her mouth, lost in the sweetness, he knew that, together, their strength would see them through hell, if necessary. Drawing back gently, lightly kissing each corner of her smiling mouth, he admitted that every day presented potential devastation. But looking into Laura's radiant blue eyes, he found the determination he needed.

As he stroked her flaming cheek, threading his fingers through the silky strands of her hair, Morgan could hardly wait to introduce Laura to his family. They would love her on sight, he knew.

The phone rang just as Laura opened the door and entered the foyer of her home. She tossed her coat and purse on the couch, having to reach over a welcoming Sasha to pick up the extension. Elated because Dr. Taggert had said that her eyes were in perfect condition, she answered the phone breathlessly.

"Hello?"

"Laura, this is Jim Woodward."

Her joy dissolved. Morgan was giving her an odd look as he came in and closed the door. "Oh, Jim…"

"Don't sound so happy to hear from me."

Rallying, Laura said, "I'm sorry. What is it you want?"

"Just to make sure you're all right. I'm still doing research on Ramsey. I'm hoping the CIA might shed some light on this for me."

She sat down, rubbing her brow. "Jim, why don't you just drop this?" Frustration built in her. Laura knew Jim's penchant for thoroughness. Often he'd accompanied her down to the photographic vaults in the basement of the Pentagon. Terror leaked through her. If Jim found photos of Morgan, he'd turn the information over to law enforcement officials. And then they would arrest Morgan.

"The guy bothers me," Woodward responded tightly. "His face... I know it! It's bugging me and I want to put all the puzzle pieces together."

Laura sighed, watching how Morgan's features had closed when he found out it was the marine captain on the phone. "Fine. You do what you want, but leave me out of it. I don't want to hear about this again, Jim. Do you understand?"

"I'm sorry I've upset you, Laura. But I've got to pursue this matter. Goodbye."

Laura put the receiver down, giving Morgan a desperate look. "That was Jim Woodward. He's still trying to identify you through photographic files and a CIA search."

Morgan nodded, his eyes hooded. "There's nothing we can do to stop him, Laura. Let's get packed. Our flight is at eight tomorrow morning. I'll take Sasha over to the kennel for you right now."

She rose, all of her happiness returning. Morgan had already agreed to bring the baby robin along in a small cardboard box. He'd assured her that his mother would love the baby bird and probably dote over it. "Okay...."

Taking Laura in his arms, Morgan gave her a game smile. He saw the worry in her eyes. "Hey, this is going to get a hell of a lot worse before it's over, Laura. If you're going to nosedive like this over one snoopy captain, what are you going to do when the heat's really applied?"

Leaning upward, Laura kissed his mouth, relishing the returning strength of his response. The thick hair from his mustache grazed her skin, sending a delightful prickle through her. "You're right," she whispered.

"I've been in tight spots before," Morgan told her, cupping her chin, gazing into her eyes. "Even if Woodward does get something on me, I'll be gone. He won't know we're in Florida because I've given the airlines an assumed name. The tracks leading to me end right here."

"I just hope he doesn't stumble onto your real name," she muttered. "Knowing Jim, he's probably going back year by year through those photo files."

"He's got seven years to plow through before he finds me," Morgan reassured her. "Come on, we've got things to do. And frankly, I can hardly wait to get home."

Chapter Seven

Morgan wiped the nervous sweat from his brow as they drove up to the Trayherns' two-story stucco home on the outskirts of Clearwater, Florida. His heart was pumping hard in his chest, and his mouth was dry as he parked the rented vehicle. He felt Laura's hand on his.

"It's going to be fine," she told him, giving him a warm smile.

"Home," he croaked. "It's just as I remember it....." Palm trees dotted the sloping landscape, and vivid red poinsettias bloomed in colorful profusion along the concrete walk and across the front of the house.

Morgan got out of the car, staring at the front door. He noticed his mother first, then his father. The shock of seeing them rooted him to the spot. All his fear dissolved at the sight of joy and welcome in their faces, not disappointment, as they hurried down the steps to the walk.

"Go ahead," Laura urged, squeezing his hand. "Go meet your parents." She gave him a little shove in their direction, following behind him.

"Oh, Morgan!" Rachel cried, throwing her arms around him.

"Mom—" He folded her tall, thin form against him, a sob tearing from deep within him. His mother was young-looking despite her fifty-six years, with the same sparkling green eyes, winsome smile and short black hair, now textured with silvery gray tones.

Laura stood back, tears in her eyes. She saw Chase Trayhern's piercing blue eyes fall first on her as he approached. Although in his early sixties, he looked much younger. His face was square, with a pronounced aquiline nose and a generous mouth that could either thin in disapproval or... He smiled a welcome to her, and Laura felt as if the sun had embraced her. Holding her hands against her heart, she felt how privileged she was to see Morgan reunited with his parents.

Chase stepped forward, throwing his arms around Morgan's broad shoulders. "It's good to have you back, son," he said, his voice quavering.

Morgan held both his parents, their heads bowed against him, all of them momentarily unable to speak.

His mother's quiet weeping, her strong, slender arms around him, broke down the last of the walls holding old grief and pain. He cried with them, time ebbing to a halt around them.

They stood locked in one another's arms for a long time. Finally Morgan raised his head, his eyes awash with tears. His voice was little more than a croak. "Laura?" He unwrapped his arm from his dad and held his hand out to her. "Come here."

She smiled unsteadily, moving forward to take Morgan's hand. Hastily wiping her tears away, she allowed him to pull her into the circle.

"Mom, Dad, you've got to meet Laura Bennett. If it wasn't for her, I wouldn't be here."

Shyly Laura held out her hand to Rachel Trayhern. Instead Morgan's mother threw her arms around Laura, hugging her tightly.

"We owe you so much," Rachel said, sniffing. "Thank you, Laura."

"Well—I didn't do much—"

Rachel pulled another handkerchief from the pocket of her green apron. "Nonsense. Here you're crying as much as I am," she said, smiling through her tears as she pressed the cloth into Laura's hand.

Blotting her eyes, Laura smiled up into Chase Trayhern's stern features. How much Morgan looked like him, she thought, as she extended her hand to him. Chase gripped it firmly, and rasped, "You've got to be quite a lady to have found our son and brought him back to us. Thank you."

Blushing, Laura was about to correct him, but Morgan interrupted.

"Let's go inside," he urged all of them. "I've got a lot of explaining to do." He gave Laura an unsteady smile as he placed his arm around her shoulders, drawing her to him.

She leaned against Morgan's strong body, deeply moved by the Trayhern family's ability to show their emotions. Somehow Laura had expected "Wolf" Trayhern to be like the other generals she'd met over the years—hard and incapable of displaying feelings. But he had Morgan's sensitivity and warmth beneath that tough skin of his. Walking at Morgan's side, Laura felt her heart lift with euphoria, because, for a while, she would be a part of this incredibly loving family.

"So that's it," Morgan said, concluding the story of what had happened to him in the past seven years. Grimly he studied his parents, who sat opposite him. Shock, disbelief, hurt and outrage showed on their faces. And that was what he felt. He glanced at Laura, who sat next to him. Straightening, he reached out, taking her hand. "And Laura thinks I can clear myself."

Chase leaned forward, a pronounced scowl on his lined face. "I can't believe Armstrong or Young would agree to smear someone like this."

"Dad, there are some officers who put their careers above and beyond honorable conduct," Morgan growled.

Rachel shook her head. "Chase, this is terrible. What are we going to do?" She got up, unable to sit still any longer.

"Take it easy, honey," Chase said soothingly. "Let's look at all facets of this problem. After the rest of the family gets here, we'll put our heads together and plan some strategy." He glanced at his watch. "Noah, Kit and their daughter, Melody, will be here in about an hour."

Morgan grinned. "Was Noah excited about seeing his big brother again?"

Chuckling, Chase rose. "'Excited' isn't the word, son. Your mother and I will get some coffee made. You and Laura just sit back and relax."

"You," Laura murmured, "have wonderful parents."

Morgan drew her into his arms. "After I remembered who I really was, I used to lie on my bunk at night, wondering how my parents would react if I walked back into their lives."

Sliding her hand against his chest, Laura laid her head against his shoulder, contentment flowing through her. "And did your dreams include this kind of welcome?"

Sifting strands of her hair through his fingers, Morgan studied her peaceful face. "I wasn't sure, Laura. I thought they might believe what the press and Pentagon had put out on me."

Each grazing touch of his fingers against her scalp increased the yearning deep within her. Laura raised her lashes, drowning in the warming gray fire in Morgan's eyes as he held her gaze. "You're like your father in many ways. The same bravery and spirit is there. And you look so much alike physically it's uncanny."

Chuckling, Morgan slid his hand down her shoulder to her arm. "Dad always said I was the spitting image of him. I got his square jaw and stubbornness."

"And your mother's warmth and sensitivity."

"You bring that out in me."

Laura sat up. "You've always had that part to you. It just got closed down because of what happened."

The urge to bring her forward and kiss her ripe lips was excruciating. But now was not the time or place. Instead Morgan brushed her cheek with his thumb. "I think you're right. Noah inherited my Mom's temperament. He's more open, more generous in showing his feelings than I ever was."

"I can hardly wait to meet him and his family," Laura said.

The momentary nervousness that spasmed through Morgan quickly abated as Noah threw his arms around him, holding him tightly for a long time before releasing him. Any doubt he'd had about his brother wondering if he was a traitor disappeared. There were tears in Noah's green eyes. Self-consciously, Morgan wiped the tears from his. He grinned, gripping Noah by his shoulders.

"It's been a hell of a long time," he rasped. He watched the tears trickle down Noah's cheeks.

"Yeah," Noah answered hoarsely. "Too long. God, it's good to see you, Morgan—" And he embraced him hard.

A sob caught in Morgan's throat as he held his younger brother for a long, poignant moment. Noah looked splendid in his uniform of light-blue shirt and dark-blue pants. Morgan felt that Noah embodied all that was good and pure and true about the Trayherns.

Gradually Noah released Morgan and stood back, wiping the tears from his face. He placed an arm around Morgan's shoulders. "Come on, I want you to meet my family."

Morgan made a point of bringing Laura to his side and introducing her to his brother. Noah's delight showed on his face immediately. And then Noah proudly brought his wife and daughter forward. Morgan warmed to Kit, who was decidedly pregnant. It was obvious that Noah and Kit were terribly in love by the tender look they shared. Their sixteen-month-old-daughter, Melody Sue, toddled confidently between the four adults during introductions.

Melody went straight to Morgan, her tiny hands barely reaching his knees, and smiled up at him. Kneeling, Morgan opened his arms to the black-haired, green-eyed little girl. Melody fell into his arms with a giggle, snuggling against him, covering his face with sloppy kisses. Tears drove into Morgan's eyes as he gently gathered Melody into his arms. She smelled so fresh and clean, her laughter light and lifting. Kissing her tiny cheek, Morgan found himself smothered with more returning kisses. Chuckling, he stood up with Melody happily ensconced in his arms.

"She's a little lover," he told Noah and Kit.

Kit's smile broadened, and she patted her swollen belly gently. "In here is Matthew Charles Trayhern. And even at six months he's showing all those famous stubborn traits you have as a family. He won't go to sleep when he's supposed to, and he keeps me up all night."

Laura leaned forward, softly stroking Melody's black hair. "She's so beautiful," she whispered. Melody stretched her arms out to her. Morgan grinned and handed her over to Laura.

"Why don't you two get acquainted?" Kit laughed. "More than anything, Melody loves to be held."

Morgan watched the play of emotions across Laura's radiant face as she took the little girl in her arms. A flush spread across her cheeks, and he saw the luminous joy in her blue eyes as she cradled the child. Looking around, Morgan savored the family that stood around him. Never, in the past seven years, had he dared dream of a moment like this. His throat constricted, he traded a grateful look with his family. They had always believed in him—never giving up on him coming back into their lives.

Noah threw his hands on his hips. "Mom, when are Aly and her husband coming in?"

Rachel brought coffee in on a tray, setting it down on the table in front of the couch. "They'll be here tomorrow afternoon." Worried, she looked over at

Morgan. "I guess now is as good a time as any to tell you about Aly's husband."

Morgan heard the anxiety in his mother's voice. "What's wrong?"

Chase came over and placed an arm around his wife. "Son, when Aly was transferred out to the naval air station near San Francisco, she got teamed up with a pilot by the name of Clay Cantrell."

Shock bolted through Morgan. "Clay? Stephen's brother?" He saw his parents nod gravely. "But—how?"

Grimly Chase said in a low voice, "We don't know. I suspect foul play at Bupers, in the Pentagon, but I can't prove it. Aly paid hell for being around Clay the first nine months of her duty. He hated her because he thought that you were responsible for his brother's death in Vietnam. And two days after the telegram arrived telling Clay's mother that Stephen had died, she had a major stroke that took her life."

Reeling from the news, Morgan shut his eyes. He felt Laura's steadying hand on his shoulder. "My God," he croaked, leveling his gaze on his father. "How did Aly survive?"

"She reached down deep into that Trayhern gene pool and hung in there," Chase growled. "They didn't have a very pretty relationship. Clay was after her to make enough mistakes to get her blackballed at first. Then they were in an air accident that they survived. They spent a week on the tip of the Baja Peninsula before they were able to get help. I guess that during that time Clay and Aly worked out their differences."

"And they're married?" Laura murmured, amazed that despite the hatred Clay Cantrell must have had for the Trayherns, love had been able to transcend the situation.

Rachel smiled. "Clay liked her from the beginning, from what he told us. He fought his attraction nearly a year. Unfortunately he let his grief and anger over what happened to Stephen and his mother interfere in his relationship with Aly. After the crash, they resolved those issues and came back here to get married."

Laura glanced up at Morgan, seeing the harshness in his eyes once again. It was a bleak look mired with pain. She tightened her hand on his arm, trying to give him solace. There would be some tense moments when Clay and Morgan met. How would Clay react? Perhaps later, when things quieted down for the evening, she could get Morgan alone, talk with him.

Laura was sitting on the wooden swing in the backyard, watching the sun set behind the wall of palm trees that defined the end of the Trayhern property, when Morgan joined her. Searching his face as he came and sat down with her, she sensed his trepidation.

"It's been one hell of a day." Placing his arm around her shoulders, he drew her against him. "How are you doing?"

She relaxed, savoring the quiet time with him. "I'm doing fine."

"Happy?"

"Very."

Morgan pushed the swing so that it moved gently back and forth. "Noah's got a beautiful wife and little girl, doesn't he?"

"Yes. They're very happy."

"I'm glad for him. After he told us about how he and Kit met, I realized just how much he'd gone through."

"Life's never easy on anyone," Laura said wryly, glancing up at him. His eyes were shadowed. "You're worried about meeting Clay, aren't you?"

Nodding, Morgan managed a cutting smile. "I'll tell you something. The stain Armstrong and Young placed on me has sullied my family even more than me. None of us has escaped the pain they've caused."

Laura heard the resolve in his voice and exulted at his determination to clear his name. "Going back to D.C. to start unraveling this mess will take priority," she stated.

"You bet it will." With a sigh Morgan leaned over and pressed a kiss to her hair. "Someone's going to pay for all the torture my family has undergone. And soon."

A little shiver of fear wound through Laura as she watched the sky turn from a brilliant orange to a blood red. The tension in Morgan's voice made his words a ground-out promise. Now she would be witness to the famous Trayhern fighting style.

"Do you know that 'Trayhern' is Welsh for superiron or superstrength?"

"No."

"Yeah, it means someone with superior strength and endurance. And I'm going to need all the genes I've inherited to uncover this frame-up."

"I think your father is planning a family conference on what to do, after Aly and Clay arrive."

Giving her a slight hug, Morgan muttered, "First things first, though. Somehow I have to convince Clay Cantrell that I didn't desert his brother and leave him to die on that godforsaken hill."

Although Clay Cantrell was dressed in civilian dark-brown slacks and a white shirt, Morgan could see the military bearing of his brother-in-law. Aly burst through the door, throwing her arms around Morgan, crying. He mussed her short red hair, kissing her damp cheek, but his eyes never left his brother-in-law, who stood stiffly at the entrance to the house.

Aly wiped the tears from her eyes, holding out her hand to her husband. "Clay, I want you to meet my brother, Morgan." Her voice was husky with feeling. "And I want you two to shake hands and *not* fight!"

Morgan made the first move, thrusting out his hand to the naval officer. He was aware of the set of Cantrell's mouth and the unsureness in his eyes. "Stephen talked a lot about you, Clay," he offered, holding his hand out to him. "We were the best of friends."

Hesitantly Clay took his hand. "You and I need to talk," he said. "Somewhere private."

Laura heard the edge to Cantrell's voice and saw the fear in Aly's face. There was so much naked emotion on the surface of each man's face that she ached for both of them. Rachel Trayhern came forward and gave Clay a hug.

"Why don't you and Morgan go take a walk in the backyard? There's a swing out there. Go sit down and resolve your differences. I'll have lunch ready in about an hour."

Relief sizzled through Laura as Rachel defused the explosiveness that surrounded the two men. Morgan glanced over at her, then turned, heading toward the back door, with Cantrell not far behind.

Laura stood there alone, watching them disappear out the door. She clasped her hands, realizing they were icy cold with nerves. Aly Trayhern came over, giving her a weak smile.

"Mom says you know everything that happened. Maybe we could sit down somewhere and you could fill me in."

Gripping Aly's hand, Laura pointed toward the living room. "Sure. Let's go in there."

It was noon when Laura finished her explanation.

The woman pilot sat there, her face devoid of color. She knotted her fists and sat up. "I can't believe this!" she cried softly. "How could they frame Morgan like that?"

"Worse," Laura murmured, "is how Armstrong and Young's decision has affected every one of you."

Rubbing her face tiredly, Aly muttered, "Our family won't let them get away with this. I promise you, we won't." Aly glanced over at her. "It's obvious Morgan couldn't have contacted us without your support."

"Well—uh—"

Her eyes narrowing, Aly studied Laura. "You won't give yourself the credit you deserve. Why?"

"It isn't necessary. What's important is Morgan, and helping him during this time."

A grin spread across Aly's features. "So there is something serious between the two of you. I thought I sensed it."

Heat flamed into Laura's cheeks. "We've known each other less than two weeks."

Chuckling delightedly, Aly got up and stretched. "I met Clay and fell head over heels in love with him the first time I saw him! It took us nine months to admit it, but the love was there from the beginning." She leaned down and patted Laura's shoulder. "Don't worry. I'll keep what I know to myself."

"Morgan has more important things to—"

Rolling her eyes, Aly laughed. "Hey! I know this big brother of mine. I saw the look in his eyes every time he glanced at you, Laura. It's obvious to me Morgan loves you. Maybe he doesn't realize it yet, and maybe you don't, either, but it's there."

Refusing to be pulled into Aly's good-natured baiting, Laura stood. "Anyone ever accuse you of shooting straight from the hip?"

Throwing her arm around Laura, Aly grinned. "That's another one of our endearing family traits, didn't you know? Trayherns never mince words when the truth will do. Come on, I'm starved! And if my eyes don't deceive me, Morgan and Clay are coming in. Let's go meet them.''

Laura felt her heart speed up as she walked with Aly to the back door. Clay Cantrell's face was no longer tense. It was softer, perhaps relieved, if she read his expression accurately. Her gaze swung to Morgan, who gave her a game smile.

"I think they've made their peace," Aly murmured, opening the door so the men could step into the house.

"I think you're right," Laura agreed, thankful.

Morgan walked through the door first. He grinned. "What is this? Two snoopy women?"

Aly punched her brother playfully in the arm. "I'll 'snoopy' you, Morgan. Laura just got done filling me in on what happened." She went over to her husband, sliding her arm around his waist, giving him a look filled with love. "Have you two settled things?"

Clay nodded, kissing his wife's cheek. "We have."

"Everything's fine," Morgan said. He slipped his arm around Laura's waist.

Laura was constantly surprised by the fact that Morgan included her, no matter what the importance of the event. She basked in his warming look, content to be embraced by him. When she saw Aly's eyes sparkling in her direction, she avoided the other woman's knowing look.

"Soup's on!" Rachel called from the kitchen.

"Come on," Morgan told all of them, "let's eat."

The dining room was filled with laughter, joking and the pleasant clink of silverware against china

plates. Laura sat next to Morgan, absorbing the wonderful atmosphere of gaiety. The Trayhern family was
a loving one, and they included her as if she were a
member. After lunch Chase Trayhern directed them all
into the living room to discuss what could be done to
help Morgan clear his name.

"Morgan," Kit said, holding Melody in her arms,
"let me try to track down Lenny Miles. My ex-boss
over in narcotics at the Miami Police Department
might be able to get something on him through department computers."

"Miles was a drug addict," Morgan said. "I had
him under arrest at the time we were on Hill 164 because I caught him high on drugs." He glanced over
at Laura, who sat close to him. "That's probably why
he survived. He was in the bunker at the time of the
last attack."

"Miles could have been buried under a lot of those
sandbags that make up the walls of the bunker," Clay
suggested. "Maybe he hid among them so the NVA
couldn't find him and run him through with a bayonet the way they did everyone else."

"Probably," Morgan agreed sourly. He directed his
attention back to Kit, who used to be an undercover
narcotics police officer for the city of Miami. "But we
still don't know if Miles is even alive. And if he is,
which city he's in."

"Doesn't matter, Morgan," Kit interrupted.
"Chuck can run a check for us in all major cities. If
Miles is still a druggie, he's probably been arrested at

one time or another. He'll have a record. We can trace him to a city, then you can go investigate. I'm sure Chuck will see to it that you get help from local law enforcement authorities. I'll tell him you're a friend, without mentioning the fact that your name is Trayhern."

"Good," Morgan muttered. He rubbed his mustache. "Better to keep this thing, I suppose, for now."

Noah sat up, allowing Melody to climb from her mother's arms into his. "Don't shave it off until you're cleared," he warned. Looking around the room, he added, "None of us will say anything about your reappearance. For now, it's a family secret. From my end, I'm going to use the Coast Guard computers to see if Miles has been involved in any drug busts at sea. Between Kit and me, if Miles is around, we'll find him."

"That sounds hopeful," Morgan congratulated them. "Laura is going to begin sifting through mountains of unclassified documents at the Pentagon from the time of the massacre on Hill 164."

"Maybe I can use my top-secret clearance to nose around a little more," Clay suggested. He glanced at Aly. "They'd never let her into certain files knowing she's your sister, Morgan. But if I took some leave, spent some time at the Pentagon, I might be able to find something—anything—that would give us information on the people involved in this coverup."

A powerful thread of hope wound through Morgan.

"From my end," Chase said, "I'm going to put pressure on people at the Pentagon level who owe me. I doubt they'll help, but it's worth a try."

"The plan sounds solid," Morgan said. "Laura and I both agree that I'll stay at her house. You can contact me there if you stumble onto anything."

"Speaking of Laura," Chase said, directing the family's attention to her, "we owe her more than we can ever repay."

"You're a Trayhern at heart," Rachel put in quietly.

Uncomfortable in the limelight, Laura bowed her head. "Morgan proved himself by staying and helping me while I was temporarily blinded by that accident. He deserves any help I might be able to give him."

Morgan understood her innate shyness at being the center of attention. Gently he squeezed her hand. "Whether you like it or not, you're part of our family now."

Self-conscious, Laura looked at each one of them, a catch in her voice as she said, "I couldn't have wished for a better family than you. You've all been so kind to me."

Aly laughed. "Osmosis, Laura. And frankly, we're proud you're a part of our team. I think Morgan has impeccable taste."

With a groan, Noah stood. "Aly, stop meddling in Morgan's personal affairs. He's capable of handling them himself."

Laura laughed nervously along with everyone else. When she looked up at Morgan, he wasn't laughing. There was pride in his eyes and—something else. Something so tender she wanted simply to throw her arms around him and love him with all her heart.

"Laura and I are going to the beach," Morgan said, getting to his feet and pulling her upright. "Anyone want to come along?"

"I see the Pacific Ocean every day from the air station," Aly piped up. "Clay and I are beat from the jet lag. I think we'll hang around the house this afternoon."

"Noah?" Morgan asked.

"I see the Atlantic and Caribbean every day from the deck of a cutter. You two are landlocked. Go down and enjoy the beach for us."

Laura smiled in anticipation of a few hours alone with Morgan. And when she saw that very male look in his eyes, a delicious tremor of anticipation swept through her.

Chapter Eight

The water was warm, easing all the tension out of Laura's shoulders and back. She swam slowly back toward shore, with Morgan at her side. The sunlight was delicious and she allowed the powerful waves to push her forward. Her feet touching bottom, she felt Morgan's arms slide beneath her back and legs, lifting her up against him.

"Morgan!" she gasped, throwing her arms around his neck. His returning laughter flowed through her, and she pressed herself against him.

"I've got you."

Closing her eyes, Laura reached up, seeking, finding his mouth. His lips were warm and cherishing, and she tasted the saltiness of the ocean on them.

"Mmm," Morgan growled, standing in knee-deep water, "you're pure heaven, little swan." And she was, in his book. Those wide, trusting blue eyes of hers would melt even the coldest of hearts, Morgan thought as he walked to the shore and deposited Laura on the blanket.

Pushing the strands of blond hair out of her eyes, Laura lay back, Morgan beside her. "This is what we needed," she whispered, closing her eyes and absorbing the sunlight.

Placing an arm behind his head, Morgan stared up at the building cumulus clouds in the dark-blue sky. "Things are moving pretty fast, aren't they?"

"Yes," Laura said, finding his hand and holding it.

"Scared?"

"A little. You?"

"A lot."

She turned her head and looked at him. "Why?"

"If Jim Woodward exposes me before we can uncover proof for my defense, it could put you and your research in jeopardy." Morgan rolled over, resting his head on one hand. He saw shadows in her blue eyes. "You're more important to me than anything else. I don't want the law to entangle you in this, Laura."

"I'll be fine."

He smiled down at her, thinking how beautifully her neck flowed into her delicate collarbones. Tracing the exquisite length of her throat, he smoothed the droplets of water from her flesh. His hand came to rest on her shoulder.

"I noticed you enjoyed holding Melody."

A soft smile pulled at Laura's lips as she gazed up at him. "I love children."

A frown worked its way across his brow as he studied her. "Are there any plans in your life to have any?"

"I'm twenty-seven now. I figured that by thirty I'd be married and on my way to having at least two or three children."

With a soft snort Morgan said, "I never even thought of having a family." Until recently. Until he'd met Laura. The gentleness and care she possessed were rare in the world, and he marveled at her abilities. Yes, Laura would be a wonderful mother.

Moving her fingers up his arm, Laura murmured, "There was no room in your life for much of anything except survival, Morgan. How could you think of getting married, much less having a family?"

Her jaw was firm as he cupped it with his hand. "Lately a lot of things in my life have changed."

Laura was unsure how to take his cryptic comment. She met his intense gray gaze that burned with unspoken desire for her alone. "And I'm sure once we get back to Washington, they'll keep on changing. Only this time, Morgan, for the better."

"I hope you're right." He gave her a broken smile laced with longing. "Just seeing Noah and Kit with Melody made me want to have what they've already earned. That little tyke is a charmer. She's got Noah's green eyes, but she's got Kit's personality."

"A nice combination," Laura agreed. There was a hunger in Morgan. She sensed it, felt it in the curve of his fingers as they stroked her cheek and saw it in his eyes. The years of loneliness had caught up with him. And just one day with his supportive, loving family had replaced a bleak and desolate future with a richness of new dreams. She sat up, placing her arms around his neck, kissing him gently.

"First things first," she told him. "We need to get back to Washington so I can begin digging for proof of your innocence."

"Miss Laura!"

Laura smiled as she walked into one of the many archive vaults far below the main portion of the Pentagon. "Hi, Pop, how are you?"

The elderly man with the balding head smiled from where he sat at his cluttered desk. "Just fine, missy. Where you been? I understand from Captain Woodward that you had a nasty accident a few weeks ago." His thick eyebrows knitted, and he studied her. "You don't look hurt. Matter of fact, you look better than I can ever recall."

Laura stopped at Pop's desk, which was stacked with pancakes of documents waiting to be put back into various files. Picking up a pen, she signed her name to allow her access to the huge, rectangular room that housed row upon row of metal files. "I've recovered now, Pop." And she did feel happier than she could ever recall. But that was due to Morgan's undeniable presence in her life—a presence that must remain a secret for now.

"What you looking for this time?"

Laura hated to lie, but it was necessary. Straightening, she rested her briefcase on the edge of his desk. "Pop, I'm beginning research for my third book about the conflict the U.S. was involved in starting in 1960."

Cackling, Pop pushed up his wire-rimmed spectacles. His brown eyes sparkled as he slowly got up and came around the desk. "So, Vietnam's next?"

"That's right."

"What year you want to start with? 1962?"

"No...I want to start with 1970 and work back."

A little puzzled, he scratched his balding head, which shone beneath the fluorescent lights. "That was close to the end of it, missy."

Laura followed him down one long wall of files. The vault was silent except for the movement of air from a number of strategically placed fans. "I know. But I want to get a perspective on our withdrawal from Vietnam first."

He rounded one corner, then stopped at another row of files, patting one of the cabinets affectionately. "Start here, then. As you know, these are all unclassified documents having to do with any communications regarding the war."

Licking her lips, Laura peered at the small, neatly written tags on each cabinet. "I'm starting with marine corps involvement."

Pop leaned over, placing a hand against his lower back. "Down here," he said, pointing a bony finger at the last cabinet, "then up here in the next section. There are at least three hundred files."

Her heart pounded briefly. "Okay. Thanks, Pop."

Chuckling, he unlevered himself from his stooped position. "The copy machine is working if you want to make duplicates of anything you find."

"Great." Usually the copy machine was broken. Setting down her briefcase, Laura smiled at Pop. Today she had worn a pair of comfortable jeans and a long-sleeved pale-pink sweater. The vaults could get cool on occasion. "Just let me know when lunch rolls around, all right? You know how I get involved in this stuff and don't realize how much time's gone by."

Shuffling down the concrete aisle, Pop nodded. "Don't worry, missy, I'll let you know."

"Pop?"

He stopped and cranked his head in her direction. "Yes?"

"Are you expecting a lot of traffic down here this coming week?" Usually people made appointments to utilize the declassified files.

"Nah, it's going to be a quiet week, missy."

"And Captain Woodward?"

"Oh, he drops in every once in a while. Lately he's been over at the photo vaults most of the time."

Probably still trying to find out something about Morgan. Hiding her worry, Laura smiled. "Thanks, Pop. I'll see you later."

"Sure thing."

Laura waited until Pop had disappeared back to his guard-dog station at the entrance to this particular vault section. Then she opened the file cabinet, and was faced with hundreds of pieces of paper tightly squeezed into the drawer. Sitting down, she pulled the first handful of papers out into her lap. She was used to this routine, having done it for years when culling for information for a military article or for one of her popular books.

Her mind kept wandering back to Morgan, who had gone over to the main library in Washington, D.C., to dredge up any and all information on Hill 164. Tonight, when they arrived back at her house, they would compare notes.

Morgan lifted his head from the copied papers he was reading. It was 5:30 p.m., and Laura was half an hour late getting home. She appeared at the doorway, her eyes red with tiredness. Sasha bounced out of the kitchen and met her in the living room, whining her welcome, thrashing her thick tail from side to side. Laura leaned over to pat her affectionately.

Getting up, Morgan asked, "How'd your day go?"

She put her coat over a chair and brought the brief-case to the table. "So-so. Yours?"

"So-so." She looked lovely, and Morgan was pleasantly surprised as she stepped up to him and placed her arms around his neck. Laura rested her head against his chest, and he folded his arms around her, relishing her firm body next to his.

"You look beat," he murmured, brushing her hair with a kiss.

"Disappointed," Laura admitted, rubbing her cheek against the cotton shirt he wore. "I should know better, Morgan. Things like this take time. I must have read hundreds and hundreds of documents today.

Most of them were company commander reports from all over Vietnam. They're not categorized by corps areas, so it's like slogging through peanut butter.''

Laughter rumbled in his chest, and he smiled down at her. ''Peanut butter, huh?''

The warm invitation in his eyes made Laura vividly aware she was a woman. ''Yes, peanut butter. Are you hungry?''

''I am.''

Laura heard the huskiness in his voice, and realized her question had dimensions to it beyond food. She saw the amusement in Morgan's eyes and managed a wry smile. ''Maybe I should rephrase the question.''

''Maybe you should.'' Morgan felt himself growing turgid with his need of Laura. She was like a light, flexible willow within his arms. The lamp on the ceiling highlighted her blond hair, creating a halo effect about her head. There was an angelic quality to her, Morgan decided, holding her lustrous gaze. His need to make love with her dissolved in the reality of the situation. Right now, he was considered a traitor to the U.S. government. If he couldn't clear his name, there would be no future for him and Laura. And he wanted one with her. Looking deep into her wide, trusting eyes, Morgan realized she was equally serious about him.

All the reasons he should keep his distance melted as he drowned in the warmth of her blue gaze. Without meaning to, Morgan tightened his arms, pressing Laura against him, feeling her softness against his mounting hardness. A groan tore from deep within him as he saw the invitation in her eyes, in the parting of her mouth.

Breath caught in Laura's throat as she read Morgan's intent. She hadn't expected it, was completely unprepared for it as he leaned down, his mouth claiming her—the heat building and then exploding as he moved his lips hungrily against hers. His mouth devoured her, his teeth grazing her lower lip, teasing her into returning his fervent plea. A little cry of surrender arched up through her, and she sagged against him, returning his fire with equal passion. Seconds spun into timelessness as reality melted under the volcanic effects of his mouth devouring her.

Abruptly Morgan broke contact, breathing hard. His eyes narrowed on Laura's flushed features. The pulse at the base of her throat was erratic, telling him just how much his unexpected kiss had affected her. *Fool!* he berated himself, suddenly releasing her and stepping away. It should never have happened! Angrily he swung around, busying himself at the counter.

Stunned, Laura stared at Morgan's powerful shoulders and back. Her lips throbbed from the force of his kiss. Feelings of disappointment swirled amid the clamoring desire he'd suddenly released within her. Morgan was male in every sense of the word, and Laura wanted to worship his strong mouth. But feelings of shame mingled with her excruciating need. Realizing he hadn't meant for the kiss to happen at all, she moved back to the table and pulled out the photocopies she'd made. Her hands shook as she retrieved the papers.

"You might want to look at these while I get dinner." Laura heard the unsteadiness in her voice and winced. Would Morgan notice it, too? She risked everything, looking toward the counter, where he stood cutting up a green pepper.

Morgan barely allowed himself to turn his head. Sweet God in heaven, but Laura was so beautiful and unsure of herself in those moments after his embrace. Guilt tore at him. Her mouth was pouty from the strength of their kiss. Had he hurt her? He hadn't meant to, not realizing until this moment how much he'd been wanting to kiss her, love her. Clearing his throat, he growled, "Yeah, as soon as I get this salad prepared."

Swallowing at the hardness she saw in his eyes, Laura again felt the euphoria he'd given her shatter. He was sorry he'd kissed her. It had been a mistake. Her heart disagreed—she'd been wanting to kiss him, love him.... Forcing more strength into her voice, she asked, "Want some help cooking?"

"I'll finish things," he said gruffly. "Go take it easy for a while. Dinner will be ready in half an hour."

Shaken by his sudden coldness, Laura nodded. He was erecting those walls he hid behind so effectively. "Let me go change," she heard herself say in a monotone. "I'll be out in about fifteen minutes." She needed the time to splash her face with cold water and stop her senses from spinning.

"Fine," **Morgan** agreed, scowling. He watched Laura leave the kitchen, with Sasha trotting at her heels. Even the slight sway of Laura's hips enticed him. She was irresistible, he decided, forcing himself to pay attention to what he was doing. A graceful, feminine woman with the ability to help him rise above his own shadowy, uncertain world.

Fifteen minutes later Laura joined Morgan in the kitchen. She'd changed into dark-green slacks and a long-sleeved white blouse with a ruffled collar. Taking an apron from a drawer, she wrapped it around her waist. Whether Morgan wanted help or not, she needed to get rid of the nervousness she still felt after his breath-stealing kiss. Sasha came over and sat on the floor at the end of the counter, watching her mistress with adoring brown eyes.

"I found out Jim Woodward is still snooping around."

Morgan lifted his head, frowning. "Oh?"

Taking out a skillet, Laura set it on the stove. "Yes. But I guess he hasn't found anything yet, because Pop, the guy who takes care of the vault material, said he's down there when time permits."

"If he discovers who I am before we find anything—"

"We'll find it first," Laura insisted, taking two steaks from the refrigerator.

"Getting stubborn about this, aren't you?" Morgan grinned.

"Jim may be a public relations officer, but he isn't an archivist like I am." Laura placed some butter in the skillet and waited for it to melt. "Give me another couple of days with those Vietnam files, and I'll have a good idea of how they're arranged. Once I get a feel for the system, I'll be able to locate Hill 164 documents more quickly."

"Good. I'm going back to the library after dinner. They don't close until ten, and I want to keep reading and taking notes." Morgan grimaced. "They sure as hell drummed me up as a traitor for the whole mess, didn't they?"

Laura felt his pain. "Yes . . . yes, they did."

"Next week Clay is going to come and start snooping in the classified documents," he said. "Maybe, among us, we'll come up with something."

Let it be sooner, rather than later, Laura thought, placing the steaks in the skillet. Jim Woodward might be slower than her at finding items in the millions of documents kept in the vaults, but he was thorough. How many weeks would it take before she could turn up some scrap of evidence—a finger pointing in the right direction? And if she didn't, then it would be even more important for Clay to come up with something.

"I think," Clay said, looking at both Laura and Morgan, "that this might mean something." Dressed in his khaki uniform, he took off his cap and tossed it on the table. From his leather briefcase he unfolded a piece of paper and handed it to them.

Morgan rubbed his watering eyes. For the past week, he'd been spending long days and nights poring over information that Laura had collected. She leaned over his shoulder as he spread the paper out on the table so they could both read it.

"I found this in a special unclassified part of Section B," Clay explained. "If it had been classified, I couldn't have made a copy and brought it out."

"It's a memo from then General Kip Young to Richard Hadden, CIA Assistant Chief of Operations," Morgan said, his brow wrinkling.

Excitedly Laura pointed to the date. "Look, this memo was written one day after Hill 164." She knew from long experience that certain declassified files were kept in Section B. Only military officials were allowed entry to that area.

Clay leaked a small grin. "Yeah, but look what it says."

Laura reached over, one hand on Morgan's arm. She sensed the strength of his muscles beneath her fingertips, and felt once again how much she was drawn to him. "'Must initiate detailed public relations offense concerning Operation Eagle,'" she read aloud.

Morgan studied it over and over again, his fingers tightening on the paper. "Young was the general over us at the time. Armstrong was a colonel below him."

Snapping her fingers, Laura quickly got up and went over to the kitchen counter, where, over the course of the week, she had begun placing certain documents in specially numbered piles. Rummaging through one stack, she pulled out a piece of paper. Her eyes shone in triumph as she brought it over to the men.

"Look at this." She traced the words "Operation Eagle" in the document. "This is a general communiqué from Armstrong to Young three days after Hill 164."

Morgan read the long, detailed document. "Most of it has to do with taking care of the bodies of my men and getting them stateside," he said. "Operation Eagle is mentioned, it seems, only in passing."

Leaning over his shoulder, Laura read the last line of the communiqué. "'Operation Eagle has been initiated.'" She looked at Morgan. "That could mean you had already been flown to Japan."

Clay rubbed his jaw. "How can you be sure that Morgan *is* Operation Eagle?"

Straightening, Laura said, "We can't be. Not yet. But the only coherent thread I've found so far is this Operation Eagle."

"And if 'Eagle' is in reference to me," Morgan added, "then this implicates Hadden at the CIA."

"Which," Laura pointed out, "ties in with what Armstrong admitted to you on his deathbed—that the CIA was involved."

"At least you know *who*," Clay said, grinning slightly. He looked at his watch. "I don't know about you, but it's time for me to hit the sack. I've got an early flight back to San Francisco tomorrow morning."

Morgan rose, thrusting out his hand to Clay. "In two days you've done a lot. Thanks."

Clay's face became solemn. He gripped Morgan's hand. "Believe me, no one wants to see the scum who really caused this fiasco caught more than I do." A twinkle came to his eyes. "Why don't you two do a little celebrating for me? Good night."

Laura smiled as Clay rose. She went over and threw her arms around his shoulders, giving him a long embrace. "Thank you, Clay. I know how hard this must have been for you."

He hugged her back, then released her, glancing significantly over at Morgan. "Better keep this woman, Trayhern. She's real special."

Flushing, Laura whispered good night to Clay and watched him retreat to the door, leaving for his hotel. She turned, and caught the naked look in Morgan's eyes. Shaken by the intensity of his hungry stare, she gathered up the papers.

Morgan stood watching Laura. She had such long, graceful hands. She made writing a sensuous experience, he decided. His need to love her warred with his caution. The past week had consisted of late nights, early mornings and twelve-hour days of sifting through material at the library or archives. There had been no time for them.

He followed her with his eyes as she walked over to the counter to straighten the pile she had riffled through earlier. Frustration ate at him. He'd like to be able to take her out to a restaurant for dinner, but he couldn't risk being identified. And they were sitting on a time bomb, with Jim Woodward continuing his investigation.

Laura felt Morgan's gaze on her. Nervously she shuffled the papers. The past week Morgan had been moody and withdrawn. That unexpected kiss had been the reason. Still, she ached to be held and kissed by him again.

Frustration claimed Laura. Why was a kiss so wrong between them? He was acting as if it were a federal offense or something. She missed his arms, his mouth strong and hot against hers. Morgan was all the man she'd ever dreamed of—but obviously she wasn't the woman of *his* dreams. She had been a disappointment.... The pain of his rejection cut her deeply, and Laura had no defense against the relentless wall of silence Morgan used as a shield between them. Taking a deep breath, she completed her duties with the documents and turned. Morgan stood in the center of the room, his hands in the pockets of his jeans, staring at her.

Need sizzled through her, and Laura managed a weak smile. "Clay's right. It's time to hit the sack. I've got an eight o'clock start tomorrow morning."

The desire to bring Laura into his arms nearly drove Morgan to reach out. He forced his hands to stay in the pockets. "I'll drive Clay to the airport tomorrow morning, then get back over to the library."

Wistfully Laura nodded. She hesitated at the entrance to the kitchen. "Good night, Morgan."

"Good night," he said gruffly. He knew sleep would come hard to him tonight—as it had this entire past week. The knowledge that Laura slept down the hall from him, when she could be in his arms, kept him tossing and turning. Sliding his fingers through his hair in agitation, he turned on his heel. If only Noah or Kit had come up with something on Lenny Miles. If only. . .

The phone was ringing. Muttering an oath, Morgan turned over, blindly groping for the phone that sat next to his bed. What time was it? The clock on the bureau read 4:00 a.m. He checked himself from answering it. No one knew he was still at Laura's. Throwing his legs over the edge of the bed, he reached for the terry-cloth robe and shrugged it on. No phone calls came at this time in the morning unless it was important.

Stumbling out of the room, he saw Laura's door open. Her hair was in disarray around her sleepy features, but she looked hauntingly beautiful in the shadowy darkness. She was struggling to slip the robe across her shoulders, the pristine length of the gown's soft fabric making her agonizingly desirable.

"Laura?" Morgan halted a foot from where she stood.

"That was Kit. They've got a lead on Lenny Miles," she said breathlessly, coming forward and throwing her arms around him. "He's alive, Morgan!" She laughed, pressing her head against his shoulder. "Alive!"

She was warm and tormentingly feminine in his arms. The shock of her body against him made Morgan dizzy for a moment. He placed his arms around her, burying his face in her silky hair. "Did they say where he is?"

Relishing the kiss he placed on her brow, Laura eased away from him, looking up into the dark planes of his face. "New York City. Skid row. Kit said they just got the information back from the N.Y.P.D. She's been using the computer at the Miami Police Department every night, searching for him. It was the only time her ex-boss would let her use it. That's why she called at this ungodly hour. Lenny has been in and out of jail on charges of drug trafficking up there since 1970."

Morgan smoothed the chenille robe against her shoulder. "Ever since Hill 164."

Excited, Laura nodded. "Kit's sending the information up by courier. We should get it no later than tonight. Oh, Morgan, I'm so excited about what this could mean!"

A slight grin curved his compressed mouth. Framing Laura's sleep-ridden face, he looked deeply into her dancing blue eyes. "It's a good idea," he admitted thickly. At one time clearing his name was the only thing that was important to him. Now, looking into Laura's hope-filled features, Morgan was reminded by the soft smile on her lips that she was equally essential to him. His fingers tightened on her flesh. "You're just as important to me, Laura."

Shaken by the huskiness in his voice, she nodded. "I know, Morgan."

"I don't know about you, but I'll be damned glad to have this behind us." Her lips were tempting, and Morgan steeled himself not to kiss her.

Laura read the torture in his eyes. He was so close, so brazenly male, that she wanted to acquiesce to the burning desire she saw in his gaze. Frustration, like a knife, cut through her. Every fiber in her body screamed for more than just casual contact with him. She couldn't forget the branding, heated kiss that had brought her own deep need to the boiling point. Just seeing the outline of his pursed mouth, remembering the strength and taste of him, made her pulse bound. There was so much they could share. Why wouldn't he? What was he afraid of? "Let's get back to bed," she said, her voice barely above a whisper. "There's no sense in losing more sleep. Now that we've found out where Lenny Miles is, everything is going to speed up."

Gently releasing her from his grip, Morgan knew she was right. "Get some sleep, then, little swan."

She continued to stare up at the craggy features of his hard face. There was such tenderness in his eyes now. "Y-yes...."

Turning, she padded back to bed, first closing the door quietly behind her. Laura leaned against it a moment, her knees feeling terribly shaky. "That man could melt steel with his look," she muttered, shedding her robe. Much less melt her heart—her soul. Pulling the covers across her, she dropped her head to the pillow, wildly aware of her heart beating in her breast. "Steel," she fumed. "He melts *me* every time we get around each other!'' With that she turned on her stomach and buried her head in the pillow, hoping to escape her clamoring needs for Morgan.

Chapter Nine

It's here," Laura said excitedly, watching as the courier van pulled into her driveway. Glancing at her watch, she saw it was five o'clock. She felt Morgan's presence behind her. The day had dragged for both of them at their respective places of research.

"The package is in your name," Morgan told her. "I'll stay out of sight."

Opening the door and exchanging brief courtesies with the driver, she signed for the hefty packet. Closing the door and turning, she handed it to Morgan. There was a new light burning in his dark-gray eyes.

"Let's go to the kitchen and see what Kit's sent us," he said, putting his arm around her shoulders, then chastising himself for the automatic response to Laura.

Cherishing the unexpected contact with Morgan, Laura leaned against him for a brief moment before pulling away. She led him to the kitchen table. Sitting down, she couldn't contain her excitement as he opened the package.

Morgan's eyes narrowed as he picked up a sheaf of copies. On top was a black-and-white photo of Lenny Miles. He snorted softly. "I wonder if I've changed as much as he has," Morgan said, turning the photo around so Laura could see it.

She studied it. "He looks like a mouse of sorts." Miles's face was triangular, his chin narrowing to a point. His eyes were small and dark, set closely together. The mouse image was emphasized by buck teeth that had never been corrected with braces. Laura almost felt sorry for him. Almost.

"He looks like someone strung out on drugs, doesn't he?" she murmured.

"Yeah. Same face I remember, but with a lot more lines." Morgan began to read the rap sheet on Miles. "He's in New York City. No known address. Kit says on a note attached that he's probably down on skid row, making one of the back alleys or a basement his home."

"That means we'll have to put in a lot of footwork."

Morgan shot her a look. "There's no 'we' to this, Laura. You aren't going into that scummy rat hole looking for Miles. That's my job."

"Hold on. You're not leaving me behind on this. We're partners. Everything we've done so far, we've done together, Morgan."

"It's too dangerous."

"Baloney."

Morgan sat up. He was getting another taste of Laura's stubborn nature. Only this time it was aimed directly at him. "You're not a cop. And you're not trained to deal with that kind of environment. I am."

Laura set her lips, her eyes blazing. "Morgan, I'm not staying behind! You may need me. I can be a second set of eyes and ears as we walk those alleys."

She was beautiful when she was angry. Morgan almost said it, but caught himself in time. Trying to keep his voice soothing, he said, "I've got eyes in the back of my head from six years in the Legion. Look, I'm going into an area where drug addicts and pimps make a living, Laura. They don't care who they put a gun to or slip a knife between the ribs of, if they're hunting for money. You'd be at risk, and I won't have it."

Clenching her hand, Laura asked, "What if you get into trouble?"

"I can handle it."

It was her turn to snort. "Give me a break! You're a marine officer. You know the value of teamwork. No one does anything alone. Even recon marines, the elite of the corps, go in teams. Quit ignoring one of the basic rules of combat, Morgan! Just because I'm a woman doesn't mean I'm a liability."

There were silver flecks of ire in her eyes. He hadn't counted on Laura using her military knowledge as a lever against his orders. "I said no."

"Damn you!" Laura got up and began pacing the kitchen. She glared at Morgan. "All those years in the Legion must have made you stupid," she ranted.

"Why you—" Morgan got up and stepped in front of her.

Laura threw her hands on her hips, her chin jutting out at a defiant angle. "You've been alone so long, you've forgotten how to be a team member, Morgan Trayhern!" Jabbing a finger into his chest, she went on, "You forget, I was raised as a military brat. I'm extremely self-reliant and able to take care of myself. You can't make me stay behind. I'm going whether you like it or not!"

He almost wanted to strangle her by her long, beautiful neck. But another part of him wanted to love her, to tap into that beckoning fire that radiated from within her. His anger and pride melded with his desire for her. Gripping her by the shoulders, he gave her a little shake. "Dammit, you're not going," he rasped. He leaned down, his face inches from hers. "Did it ever occur to you that I like the hell out of you and don't want to see you get hurt?"

Tears flooded Laura's eyes and she forced back the reaction. Morgan's hands were branding on her shoulders. "I like you enough to go along whether you want me to or not!"

Something snapped within Morgan. With a growl he brought Laura hard against him. Crushing his mouth to hers, he meant to subdue her. Instead her lips parted, allowing him entrance, and he tasted the sweetness of her depths. All his anger melted as her hungry response shattered his resolve. Her arms slid upward, moving against his neck. The feminine scent unique to her entered his flared nostrils, and he inhaled deeply, lost in his need of her. The world ceased to exist for him as she pressed against him. Laura was pure sunlight flooding his dark existence. Needing her, wanting to satisfy the sharpened ache in his lower body, he slid his hands roughly down and across her small shoulders, finding and fitting her breasts into his hands.

A moan escaped him as her flesh became firm beneath his cupping motion. Fire, more violent and seething than he'd ever experienced, erupted deep within him. He could feel the tautness of her nipples beneath the fabric of her blouse. Laura was so warm, so willing. . . .

Just as suddenly Morgan realized what he was doing. He fought the drugging beauty of her mouth, now wet and inviting. It hurt to break contact with her sweet lips. Bare inches separated them, and Laura's eyes were lustrous and dazed. Even more reason to keep her safe from harm, his mind screamed at him.

"You're such a little hellion when you want to be," Morgan grated. Just holding her shoulders to reinforce what he said had a pleasurable effect upon him.

Dizzied by the unexpected ferocity and primal need of Morgan's kiss, Laura stammered breathlessly, "I'm going."

Her lips were pouty, beckoning. He could kiss them again. Laura was so close, and the ache intensified within him. All his anger backwashed. "Didn't you hear me? I care for you, Laura...."

"And trying to make me feel guilty isn't going to work, either, Morgan!" His male scent did nothing but increase her womanly awareness of him. There was an animal gleam in his narrowed eyes. He was the hunter and she was his quarry. Excitement thrummed through Laura as her attention wavered between their words and the heated looks they were trading. Laura didn't want to argue. She wanted to make hungry, passionate love with Morgan. Her voice cracked. "I care for you, too! How can I stay here worrying for days or weeks about you? I couldn't stand the nightmares I'd have of you stabbed in some dark alley." Laura tore from his grasp, pleading with him. "There won't be any police backup. You'll be alone. I'm not about to let you walk into this mess without me at your side."

Hanging his head, Morgan felt Laura's anguish. Even more, his senses cried out as she pulled from his grasp. He wanted to explore that bounding pulse at the spot where her graceful neck intersected with her small but proud shoulders. Giving himself a mental shake, Morgan tried to still his savage want of her. He knew what it was like to be alone. So damned alone. One look into her blue eyes, and he couldn't tell her no. "It won't be easy, Laura. I plan on being out on the street all day and part of the night."

A weakness stole through Laura. She gripped the back of the chair to steady herself. The naked look in Morgan's eyes had stripped her, was making silent love with her. It was so hard to concentrate! Finally, struggling to sound coherent, Laura whispered, "I'll wear sensible shoes, then."

An unwilling grin tugged at the corners of his mouth. "Who could ever believe there was such a spirited hawk beneath that guise of swan you wear?"

Rubbing her arms because she was suddenly cold, Laura shrugged. "I care enough to be with you, Morgan."

"This isn't going to be fun. And there will be danger."

She lifted her chin, holding his suddenly bleak look. All the fire had died in his eyes, leaving only embers of an unfulfilled promise between them. She felt his emptiness just as sharply as she felt her hunger for him. "Together we're strong, Morgan."

With a sigh, he turned back to the table and sat down, making an attempt to concentrate. But how could he? Laura's voice was like a caress. Her eyes promised him a velvet world of love anytime he wanted to take her into his arms. Rummaging through the rest of the background information on Lenny Miles, trying to get a grip on his turmoil of emotions, he rasped, "We're going to have to be."

Even the grate in Morgan's voice was like his hand brushing her sensitized skin. Everything in her responded to his dark tone. Laura closed her eyes, fighting off the wave of dizziness. "I'll call the airlines and make reservations for a flight to New York tomorrow morning,'' she answered, her voice wispy with barely contained emotion.

Worried for her already, Morgan nodded, saying nothing. His mind and heart swung to Laura's safety. Anything could and did happen in those alleys. There was roving street gangs, kids who wielded knives and guns as easily as he had in the Legion. Only they weren't adults, just children. Rubbing his face tiredly, Morgan closed his eyes. His life took on new importance because of Laura. And there was no way in hell he was going to lose her. No way....

The wind tugged at Laura's overcoat, and she pulled the collar up, protecting her exposed neck. New York at nine o'clock on Monday morning was windy and cold. Eyes focused straight ahead, Morgan appeared impervious to the vicious wind that tore at his dark brown leather jacket, jeans and work boots. He looked like a construction worker. Or perhaps a grim soldier with a mission to accomplish.

She was getting a taste of his other side now. The side that had survived Hill 164 and the Legion. There was no forgiveness in Morgan's set features as his narrowed gray gaze roved down the street. Shivering, she hurried to keep up, feeling sympathy for the drunks who lay on the sidewalk. At each one Morgan would stop. If the person was conscious, he'd pull out a photocopied picture of Lenny Miles and ask if they knew him.

An alley came into view. Morgan halted, searching the trash-scattered depths of the area. Spotting someone lying by a dumpster, he walked in that direction. All the time his senses were screamingly alive. The wind tugged at him, and he bowed his head slightly. Rain was coming, and soon, judging from the darkening clouds above the city.

Leaning down, Morgan tapped the man in the soiled wool coat. "Hey, buddy, are you awake?"

The man growled a curse, slowly unwrapping from a fetal position. He looked up, his eyes red and watery. "What you want?"

Morgan pulled out the picture of Miles from his pocket. "I'm looking for someone." He placed the picture in front of the bloodshot eyes of the drunk. "You ever seen this guy? His name is Lenny Miles."

The drunk rolled back over and curled up. "Get outa here. I ain't seen 'im."

Straightening, Morgan perused the rest of the alley. It was empty. He glanced at Laura. The compassion on her face gripped his heart. Taking her by the arm, he turned her around and headed back out the alley.

"You're not going to make it," he told her tightly.

"I will, too!"

"You're ready to cry."

"So what?" Laura jerked out of his grip, glaring up at him. "Since when can't I feel for these street people? It's cold and windy out here. That old man didn't have enough clothes on to keep him warm. He was shivering!"

Morgan couldn't stand the fact that he'd brought tears to her eyes. He and Laura had been pounding the pavement for almost two hours since their arrival. He'd gotten them two rooms at a hotel not far from skid row, and they had left shortly thereafter to begin the hunt.

"Laura, you aren't cut out for this," he said patiently, walking back toward the street.

"Who is?" Laura shot back, giving him an accusing stare. "You can't tell me you enjoy this. Or that you don't feel sorry for these people."

"We all have our personal hells to deal with," he muttered.

Laura choked in a breath. He was right: the sight of those destitute and helpless people was tearing her up. Somehow she was going to have to steel herself against their misery long enough to help Morgan. She saw the frustration and anger in his eyes.

Morgan glanced up at the sky. "It's going to start raining like hell in a minute." He took in her pale face, her eyes that burned with stubbornness. "Sure you don't want to go back to the hotel?"

"No. As long as you're out on the street, I'm staying with you."

"Okay, wingman, let's get going."

She managed a one-cornered smile at his use of the term *wingman*. No fighter pilot flew without another fighter beside him. It was a protective measure. As they headed deeper into skid row, Laura began to see street gang members; two or three young men wearing the symbol of their gang on the backs of their jackets. There was a tension in Morgan, and suddenly Laura was grateful for his military training and abilities. This was no place for a woman alone.

The rain began violently with huge drops exploding like minibombs all around them. Laura shielded her eyes with her hand. Morgan simply hunched more deeply into the jacket, pulling up the collar to protect the back of his neck. The streets began to clear.

Halting at a basement tavern, Morgan pulled her close beside the ramshackle establishment to protect her from the storm. The paint was peeling off the front and the window was caked with grease and dirt. Frustration thrummed through him. Laura had no business being here! She was like a beautiful lily in the midst of a garbage pile. He tightened his fingers on her arm.

"We're going into this joint. Stick close."

Nodding, she followed on his heels as he opened the creaking door. Clouds of cigarette smoke and the odor of stale alcohol hit her sensitive nostrils. It took precious seconds for her eyes to adjust to the smoky gloom within the tavern. Laura pressed herself against Morgan's back, feeling eyes upon her. There were men and women sitting at round wooden tables, talking in lowered voices. The pungent scent of unwashed bodies assailed her as she moved forward with Morgan toward the bartender behind the counter.

Morgan pulled out the photo, thrusting it under the heavyset bartender's bulbous red nose. "I'm looking for this guy. His name is Lenny Miles. You seen him?"

Scratching his balding head, the bartender took the photocopied picture and held it up to better light.

Morgan felt Laura's hand around his upper arm. She was frightened. Who wouldn't be in a dive like this? The only people in there were drunks or drug addicts, judging from the blankness in their slack, sallow faces. He wanted to soothe her fears, but there was no way to do it. Gazing down the bar, he saw a thin-faced young man in his middle twenties watching them with interest. The man was dressed in a gray silk suit, out of place among the rags worn by the other patrons. He must be a pimp.

"I dunno," the bartender said, placing the photo on the counter. "Sure looks familiar... wha'dja say his name was?"

Morgan divided his attention between the pimp looking Laura over and the bartender. "Lenny Miles. He's a drunk and a drug addict."

Rubbing his nose, the bartender peered down at the picture. "Give me a minute, Mac. I mighta seen him, but I gotta remember."

"Take your time," Morgan said. He stiffened inwardly as the pimp came strolling around the bar directly toward them.

Laura's eyes widened as the man in the suit walked up to her, grinning. She shrank back against Morgan, disgusted by the leer in the man's dark brown eyes.

"Nice filly ya got there, fella. But I gotta tell ya, this is my turf. Nobody does business in here without Rico's permission." He reached out to touch the blond hair lying against Laura's shoulders.

Morgan shot out his hand, capturing Rico's arm in a viselike grip. "Back off, punk, or you'll regret it," he snarled.

Laura uttered a little cry and stumbled backward, hitting a table. She straightened, her hand across her mouth. Rico's thin face went livid as he glared up at Morgan.

"Get your hand off me," Rico sputtered.

"Leave the lady alone."

Rico snorted. "Hey! She's just another piece of meat to sell, buddy. You ain't movin' in on my turf!"

The urge to put his fist right through Rico's snarling face was tempting. With a grin Morgan shoved Rico away from him. The pimp crashed into another table, then fell to the unswept wooden floor.

Laura gave a small cry of warning as she saw Rico scramble to his feet, drawing a knife from beneath his gray silk suit coat.

"She's mine," Rico whispered, holding the knife outward.

Morgan's eyes glittered. Grabbing a beer bottle, he smashed it against the counter, keeping the jagged remains as a weapon in his hand. He kicked a chair out of the way, then stood in a wide stance for better balance. "No way, punk. The lady's no hooker, and she isn't for sale." The pimp leaped forward, knife hand extended. In one swift motion Morgan lifted his foot, his boot coming into hard contact with Rico's wrist. The pimp cried out as his weapon sailed out of his hand.

Breathing harshly, Morgan caught Rico as he fell off balance from the kick he'd delivered. Grabbing the pimp by the collar of his suit, he slammed him head-first into the counter. With a groan Rico slumped to the floor, holding his bloodied nose.

"Now get the hell out of here," Morgan snarled, leaning down and jerking Rico back to his feet.

Laura watched as Morgan threw Rico out the front door, then slammed it shut after him. Dizziness assaulted her, but she caught herself, gripping the table for support. She heard snickers from the patrons.

"You all right?" Morgan asked, coming over to her.

"Y-yes, fine."

He cocked his head, studying her darkened eyes and pale skin. "You don't look very good. Here, sit down." Pulling out a chair, he guided Laura over to it.

"Hey, Mac," the bartender called, waving Morgan back over to the counter. "I think I remember now. They call him 'Lenny the Rat.'"

Hesitantly Morgan left Laura's side. She looked as if she were going to faint. "Tell me what you know about him," he ordered, wiping his hands on the thighs of his jeans. Everything about this place was seedy and dirty.

"Not much to tell ya. Lenny's like most of 'em. He sleeps during the day and gets active at night."

"There's a bunch of flophouses about five blocks from here, but it's a real rough area. Even the cops don't go in there unless it's with a couple of cruisers—and then only after a murder's been committed.'' The bartender rubbed his almost nonexistent chin. He studied Morgan for a moment, then grinned. ''But I got a feelin' you can take care of yourself. Anybody who can take on Rico, can take on Hombre.''

''The local gang leader?'' Morgan guessed.

''Oh, yeah. But Hombre's nasty as they come.''

''And you think Lenny the Rat might be over on his turf?''

''I'm pretty sure. He's one of Hombre's dealers, if I remember right.''

''Thanks,'' Morgan said with feeling. He picked up the photo and put it back in the pocket of his plaid shirt. Turning, he focused his attention on Laura. She was completely out of her environment, while he had spent hours at dives like this, thinking and alone.

''Hey, Mac,'' the bartender called. ''You'd better get her outa here. She ain't gonna make it here. Ya know what I mean?''

Grimly Morgan nodded. ''Yeah, I understand. Thanks.''

Laura stood as Morgan approached. His tense face softened, and she longed simply to fall into his arms. Fighting all her needs, she stood on her own.

''I heard what the bartender said.'' She heard how strained her voice sounded and she strengthened it. ''Wouldn't it be safer to go over and check out those flophouses in daylight?''

Looking around, Morgan saw that every patron was watching them with unparalleled interest. He gripped her arm and led her to the door. They'd do their arguing outside. "Come on," he told her.

Outside the tavern, the wind tore away the smell hovering around her, and Laura appreciated the cleansing rain. She stood huddled next to the tavern wall, her hands shaking so badly she couldn't hide it from Morgan.

Morgan moved behind her to shield her from the driving wind and rain. Water ran in rivulets down his drawn features. "I'm taking you back to the hotel," he growled. "There's no way in hell you're following me into Hombre's territory."

"I'm going, Morgan." There was an edge to her voice, and Laura watched him react to it.

Words were useless and he knew it. Capturing her hand, he pulled her around, heading back toward the hotel. The rain slashed at him, and he lowered his head. Laura tried to jerk out of his grasp. Dammit, he didn't want to hurt her!

"Stop fighting!" he growled, throwing his arm around her shoulders and bringing her against him.

Tears of anger mingled with the cold rain. Her hair wilted around her face, becoming wet ropes. Morgan's strength was too much for her, and she acquiesced, burying her head against his shoulder.

Their middle-class hotel sat on the edge of the skid row district. Laura was soaked to the skin by the time they arrived at their rooms. Morgan took her key, opened her door and led her inside.

"You're shaking like a leaf," he muttered, throwing his jacket onto a chair. "Come here."

Her teeth were chattering, and Laura allowed him to unbutton her trench coat and peel it off her. She was cold, yes. But fear was making her reaction worse. Grateful for Morgan's hand on her elbow, she let him guide her to the bed, and she sat down.

"I-I'm so cold," she whispered as he knelt to pull the soaked shoes from her feet.

Morgan shot her a knowing look. "You're more scared than cold."

Gripping her hands in her lap, Laura hung her head. "Weren't you frightened when Rico pulled that knife on you?" Off came her socks. Then Morgan got to his feet and pulled her upward.

"No."

Laura started to protest when he began to briskly unbutton her yellow blouse. The material clung to her goose-bumped flesh. "Wh-why?" Each time his fingers grazed her, her skin tingled beneath his touch.

Morgan drew the soaked blouse off her shoulders. His scowl deepened as he threw it on the bed. "Because the punk didn't even know how to hold a knife properly. Sit down."

Numbly Laura obeyed, hotly aware of Morgan's burning gaze on her breasts. Even the silky bra she wore was wet. He unbuttoned and unzipped her jeans, pulling them off her, one leg at a time. Unable to speak because her teeth were chattering, Laura watched as he dragged her chenille robe from her suitcase.

"Get this on. I'm going to start a hot shower for you. You're freezing."

"N-not a shower. I-I don't think I can stand up."

Morgan nodded. "All right, a hot bath." He saw her fumble awkwardly with her robe, her hands shaking.

"Come here," he said huskily, getting her to stand. He helped her on with the robe, wildly aware of the feminine lingerie she wore. It was the first time he had seen her without clothes, and she was beyond his most heated, passionate dreams. Fighting his desire to drag her into a hot shower with him, he closed the robe with the sash, then forced her to sit back down on the bed.

Laura closed her eyes and hunched over, trembling, on the bed. Why couldn't she be more brave? The adrenaline that had shot into her bloodstream when Rico pulled the knife had unhinged her. She had been so frightened for Morgan. Just the mere thought of him getting hurt made her blanch. She hadn't been frightened for herself but for him. Would he understand that?

Minutes later, Morgan came out of the bathroom. And with the same brisk efficiency, he led Laura from the bed to a tub that was rapidly filling with steaming hot water. He stood inches from her, his hands resting on her slumped shoulders. Gently he moved aside her tangled wet hair, grazing her pale cheek.

"Listen, you get a long, hot bath and relax. I'm going to go downstairs and order us some lunch. When you're done soaking, we'll eat here, in your room. How does that sound?" Morgan felt the heat within him threaten to overwhelm him as she lifted those long, thick lashes, her eyes dark and shadowed with fear. Her lower lip trembled. With a groan he felt his heart dissolve beneath Laura's look, pleading with him to kiss her.

Morgan's breath was warm and moist across her cheek as he leaned down to claim her. Laura trembled as his mouth took hers with hungry abandon. She fell against him, hungrily returning the branding kiss that seemed to devour her with fire. As he ran his hands up and down her back and hips, she felt herself drowning in the glory of his ardor, sweeping through her like liquid heat.

Tearing his mouth from her lips, Morgan gripped her. Both of them were breathing raggedly. Laura's lips were wet, inviting. He saw the swell of her breasts outlined by the lavender robe, the nipples pronounced, begging him to touch and tame them. How long could he continue to fight the natural beauty that came straight from her heart? Closing his eyes, Morgan gripped her shoulders hard.

"Get your bath, Laura."

She swayed in his grip, her lips throbbing in the wake of his kiss. "A-all right...."

Tearing himself away from her, Morgan headed blindly out of the bathroom, shutting the door behind him. He stood for nearly a minute, fighting his desire, fighting his primal need for her. Then, rubbing his face savagely, he forced himself to leave her room, lock the door and go downstairs to order their lunch.

* * *

Laura stared into her own eyes in the mirror. They were a soft powder blue. Her hands no longer shook as she combed through her just-washed hair. There was color back in her cheeks, but she knew it wasn't so much from the bath as from Morgan's fiery kiss that had claimed her very soul. Setting the comb aside, she applied lipstick, then dressed in a pale-pink blouse, blue jeans and dark fuchsia sweater.

There was a knock at the door. Laura answered it to find Morgan with two sacks of food in his hands.

"Come in," she said breathlessly. Even now, she could see the pewter flame burning in his eyes. She shut the door, watching him place the sacks on the small desk.

Morgan stole a look at Laura as she came over to sit down. She looked vulnerable and beautiful in the jeans and sweater. "You look better," he muttered. Did she hear the desire in his tone? He hoped not.

Laura opened the first sack and pulled out the contents. "I feel much better." It was obvious he didn't want to discuss their torrid kiss. But it was so hard to ignore his powerful masculinity and the desire in his gaze that her heart pounded with a swift staccato beat. She wasn't hungry, but she knew she'd better have something. Morgan had ordered them turkey sandwiches, French fries and coffee.

"Here, you eat first," she said, opening the second sack.

Morgan took a drink of the coffee, scalding his tongue. Damn! Staying around Laura was throwing his feelings into a tailspin. Frowning, he ate in silence. Just the way she held the sandwich in her slender fingers made him ache for her. There was nothing Laura did that wasn't sensual in his eyes.

After lunch, Morgan gathered up the sacks and wrappers. "I'm going back down there." He shot her a dark glance. "And I want you to stay here and rest."

Laura looked out the window of the hotel room. It was pouring. Just the thought of going back into that slashing, freezing rain made her shiver. She watched Morgan put the sacks into the wastebasket near the bed. His shoulders were incredibly broad, his back strong and powerful. The look on his face told her not to argue with him. "When will you be back, Morgan?"

He picked up his damp leather jacket, shrugging it over his shoulders. "I don't know."

"Please," she whispered, "don't get caught out there after dark, Morgan. Don't...."

Managing a tight smile, he came over to where she sat. "Did I tell you how pretty you look in that sweater?" He caressed her cheek longingly. "Gives color to your face."

Laura cradled his face between her hands. "Morgan, be very careful, do you hear me?" The words *I love you* were nearly torn from her. She brushed her fingers through his damp hair.

"Sweet little swan," he murmured, "I've got everything to live for now." Her lips were soft and pliant beneath his brief, searching kiss. Morgan stood. Laura's eyes were filled with anxiety and fear. "Stay here and keep the door locked. Don't open it for anyone but me. Understand?"

Laura nodded convulsively. Gripping her hands, she watched Morgan leave the room. A coldness swept through her as she sat alone at the desk. Morgan was like warming sunlight to her existence. Uttering a little cry, she pressed her hand to her brow. "I love you, Morgan." The words met a silent room in the wake of his exit. Would he be safe? What if Hombre found him? Suddenly Laura could not sit still. She got up and began pacing the rectangular expanse. Her heart ached with a new pain—one of fear for Morgan's life. He'd nearly given his life for his country once, and had been accused of being a traitor. Now he had to face a different kind of war zone to reclaim his innocence. If only he could find Lenny Miles. If only...

Chapter Ten

I'm looking for Lenny the Rat,'' Morgan told a young teenager standing just inside the door of a battered old hotel. The red-haired youth shrugged, blowing cigarette smoke out his pinched nostrils.

"Ain't here."

"Where, then?'' Morgan moved inside the hallway, on guard. The boy, who couldn't be more than sixteen, carried a knife in a scabbard just inside the leather jacket he wore.

The youth sized up Morgan with a disgusted look. "You a cop or somethin'?"

"No. I knew Lenny a long time ago, and I'm trying to find him."

"Try the next flophouse down. The Rat usually sleeps in the basement with the rest of the sleaze."

Morgan nodded. "Thanks." He went back into the rain, thrusting his hands deep into the pockets of his jacket. Miserable weather for a miserable day. But he could remember far worse monsoon rains in Vietnam. This was nothing in comparison. Walking quickly down the concrete sidewalk spiderwebbed with cracks, Morgan kept his gaze on the five-story brick structure with broken windows where Lenny might be staying.

There was a group of teenage boys huddled in the doorway of the dilapidated hotel. The windows were patched with cardboard and tape, lending to the beaten image. Pulling his hands out of his pockets, Morgan slowly walked up the steps.

"Hold it right there," a blond-haired boy warned.

Morgan halted within six feet of the group. They all wore the same style of black leather jacket with a tiger emblazoned on the back. "I'm looking for Lenny the Rat."

"What for?" the blond youth challenged, standing with his feet spread, hands on his thin hips.

"I'm a friend of Lenny's. I need to talk with him."

"Frankie, he looks like a cop," a black-haired boy growled.

The blonde grinned, confident with his cohorts surrounding him. "No cop is stupid enough to walk into Hombre's territory alone, Mickey. You lookin' to buy, mister?"

Morgan shook his head. "Drugs aren't my style."

"Then he's a cop!" Mickey cried, pointing a finger at him. "Let's cut 'im up and send 'im back to the precinct."

His eyes hardening, Morgan stared at Mickey, then at Frankie. "You start anything and I'll finish it. I'm not a cop. I'm here to find Lenny."

Frankie lifted his chin, weighing Morgan's growling rejoinder. "It'll cost ya, mister."

"How much?"

Frankie pursed his thin lips. "Say...a hundred bucks."

"Lenny's not worth more than ten bucks."

Laughing sharply, Frankie moved lithely down the stairs, his skinny hand extended. "Deal."

Taking a ten-dollar bill from his pocket, Morgan thrust it into the kid's hand. "Take me to Lenny."

"Hey, Mickey, take this dude to the Rat," Frankie ordered, stepping aside.

The rest of the gang moved to allow Morgan entrance into the flophouse. The hallways were littered with garbage and bottles. An unpleasant odor stung his nostrils. Keying one ear to the gang members who remained at the door, Morgan followed Mickey deeper into the hotel. He didn't trust any of them. He could be jumped at any time.

Mickey stopped and jerked open a door that was hanging by one hinge. "He's down there with the rest of 'em."

Nodding, Morgan moved to the rickety wooden stairs and stood for a minute, allowing his eyes to adjust to the gray light seeping through the pitifully few windows in the basement. Mickey left. Occasionally a snore, or maybe it was a groan, escaped from one of the fifteen or so sleeping figures huddled below him. He was glad Laura hadn't come along. She couldn't have handled this kind of scene.

Quietly Morgan descended into the basement. Most of the men and boys were sleeping, curled up on cardboard, or whatever they could find that was dry, to keep warm. He stopped at each person. Some remained asleep and he could tell they weren't Lenny. Others awakened as he drew near, their eyes malevolent with warning to stay away. Morgan respected their distance as he moved carefully among them.

His disappointment grew stronger with each man he checked. Finally there was only one person left, in the far corner, wrapped in a tattered and filthy olive-green wool blanket. Morgan stepped through the clutter on the floor, making his way toward the sleeping figure.

Leaning over, Morgan gripped the thin shoulder through the damp blanket. Muttering, the man turned his face, his hooded eyes puffy slits.

"Miles." The name came grinding out of Morgan. He tightened his grip on the man's shoulder, forcing him against the wall.

Lenny looked up, his eyes widening. They were glazed over, indicating he was high on drugs. "No!" he croaked, trying to scramble backward but stopped by the wall.

"Hold still!" Morgan hissed, kneeling to grab the ex-soldier by his filthy collar.

Lenny was breathing hard, his voice high and off-key. "Captain Trayhern! No! It can't be...they...they said you were—"

"Shut up, Miles. Shut up and listen." Morgan leaned forward, baring his teeth. "You and I have some talking to do, Miles. I need you to testify for me. You're going to clear my name. Now come on, get up!" He hauled the small man to his feet.

"But," Lenny squealed, "I can't! They'll kill me! They said they'd kill me if I—"

"And I'll kill you if you don't testify about what really happened, Miles," Morgan muttered savagely. He placed one hand on the addict's collar and jerked one arm behind him. "Come on, we're getting out of here."

"You can't do this!" Lenny screamed, fighting weakly against Morgan's superior strength and bulk.

"Like hell I can't. Now move it, Miles." He pushed him toward the stairs.

Lenny Miles was in a weakened state that alarmed Morgan. The guy was nothing but skin hung over bone. He'd gone downhill since Morgan had last seen him. Guiding Miles toward the entrance, Morgan saw that the Hombre gang had disappeared. Good. It would make his job easier getting Miles safely back to the hotel.

As he dragged Miles out of the house and onto the street, Morgan wondered how Laura would react to this disheveled man who had knowingly put the name "traitor" on him.

The heavy, persistent knock at her door sent Laura into a spasm. She leaped off the chair, running to answer it.

"Who is it?"

"Morgan. Meet me over in my room, Laura."

"Okay." She took the key from her purse and quickly opened the door, then walked out into the carpeted hall. Morgan's door was open. As she entered his room, a stench assailed her, and she winced. When she saw Lenny Miles sitting unhappily on a wooden chair, she came to a halt.

Morgan kept a hand on Miles, not trusting him. "This is Lenny Miles," he told her darkly.

Compassion swept through Laura as she stared at the unkempt, thin man. Lenny really did look like a frightened mouse.

"Let me go, Captain," he wailed. "I don't know nothin'!"

"Shut the door, Laura," Morgan ordered grimly.

Lenny cringed when Morgan lifted him to his feet. "You're sickening, Miles." He shoved up the sleeve on the threadbare jacket Lenny wore. There were at least ten needle tracks, attesting to his shooting hard drugs. Turning, Morgan told Laura, "Get a bath ready. I'm going to scrub him until he squeaks. While I'm doing that, you go downstairs to the men's store and buy him some decent clothes."

Nodding, Laura did as he asked. In no time the bath was prepared. She laid out several towels, a fresh bar of soap and a razor. Lenny was stinking and dirty.

That scraggly brown beard did nothing but make him appear more gaunt.

"The bath's ready, Morgan," she called.

Morgan had already stripped Miles of everything but his trousers. "Thanks. Now go get those clothes. You can take his filthy garments with you."

Laura had never seen Morgan in this kind of a mood. His face was hard, and so were his eyes. This was his soldier side, the fighter side. "I'll throw them in a paper sack," she said quietly.

"After you get the clothes, put them in my room and then go to yours until I call you," he ordered, dragging Lenny toward the bathroom.

Relieved that Morgan was safe and unharmed, Laura nodded and left. From the look on his face, he was ready to drown Lenny instead of wash him. Her hands shaking, she clutched the filthy remains of Miles's clothes and made her way back to her room. She was sure that as soon as Morgan got him decent, he'd begin interrogating him. A cold shiver rippled up her spine. With the mood Morgan was in, he could hurt Lenny Miles badly.

An hour later Morgan called her. He wanted the tape recorder brought over. Grabbing it, Laura left her room and walked those few feet down the hall. The door to Morgan's room was open, and she stepped inside. Morgan looked agitated, his sleeves rolled up on his forearms, the front of his shirt damp from Miles's much-needed bath.

"Laura, you ready with that tape recorder?"

She nodded, placing the microphone on the desk next to where a miserable Lenny Miles sat. "Ready."

Morgan took the other chair, turned it around and threw a leg over it. He sat down only a few feet from Lenny. Dressed in a white shirt and brown trousers, his face scraped clean of a beard, Miles looked almost presentable. Already his hands were beginning to shake because he was coming off the high.

Following standard police procedure, Morgan made Lenny give his full name, present address, then his military rank and where he'd been stationed back in 1970. After Lenny had stammered through the obligatory answers, Morgan pounced on him. "All right, Miles, I want to know what Armstrong and Young put you up to after the massacre on Hill 164."

Standing to one side, Laura made sure the tape was recording properly. She saw the naked fear in Lenny's small, dark eyes. He wrung his hands.

"Look, Captain, I can't say anything! If I do, they'll kill me."

"And I'll kill you if you don't. My life's at stake, Miles. You've helped mess up seven years of it. Now I want the truth."

Lenny hung his head. "Please," he squeaked, "they'll kill me!" Then he added imploringly, "Look, I gotta have a fix or I'm gonna lose it!"

Morgan was about to reach forward and jerk Miles up by his collar, when Laura placed her hand on his shoulder. He glanced at her. There was pain in her blue eyes.

"Let me try," she pleaded.

His nostrils flaring, he nodded.

"Lenny, my name is Laura Bennett. I'm a military archives expert from Washington, D.C."

Gradually Lenny came out of his crouch and raised his head. "The Pentagon?"

"That's right. Certain information was given to Morgan about why he was blamed for Hill 164. General Armstrong himself told Morgan the truth."

Lenny's eyes grew round. "He did?"

"That's right," Laura said, keeping her voice quiet and calming. "Don't you think that if General Armstrong told Morgan the truth, you can tell us what you remember about the plan?"

Chewing on almost nonexistent fingernails, Lenny gazed at the floor for a long time.

Morgan sat tensely. If only Laura could drag the truth out of Lenny. He wanted to wrap his hands around the bastard's neck and wring his life out of him for what he'd done.

Gently Laura squeezed Lenny's shoulder. The man jumped like a frightened mouse. She gave him a pleading smile. "We know about Operation Eagle, Lenny."

He gasped. "Eagle? They told you about Eagle?"

"We know that a CIA chief by the name of Richard Hadden approved the operation."

"Well—I don't understand," he wailed. "If you know all this, you know everything!"

"You see," Laura whispered, trying to get him calmed down again, "we have most of the information. All that's missing is your reason for getting into this mess, Lenny.''

He glanced up at her. ''Well—I, uh, didn't plan on it.''

''I know. You were under arrest and in a bunker when the NVA attacked the hill for the last time,'' Laura began, hoping he'd continue the story.

''Yeah...well, I was.'' He glanced apprehensively at Morgan. ''The captain saved my life by having me down in that bunker. I was high on drugs and couldn't have hit the broadside of a barn with my M-16.'' He grimaced. ''A rocket hit the bunker and the next thing I knew, I was buried among hundreds of sandbags. That's what saved me, ya know?''

''I'm glad it did. What happened next, Lenny?'' Laura coaxed.

''I don't know how long it was before marine reinforcements reached Hill 164. When I heard American voices, I started screaming for help. They dug me out. Colonel Armstrong was there, and he wasn't happy. They took me aside and told me I was the only survivor. The colonel said he wanted me in solitary back at battalion headquarters so he could interrogate me.''

''You're doing fine,'' Laura praised him.

Lenny peeked at Morgan's grim features, then returned his attention to Laura. ''I was in solitary for an entire day. The next morning, Armstrong came in with General Young. I repeated what I knew. He told me you were the cause of the massacre. At the time I didn't know any different. I was in the bunker and didn't see anything. And if I went along with their

story, they said they'd give me the drugs I wanted."
Licking his lips, Lenny blurted, "I needed a fix real
bad. They didn't have to twist my arm very hard to get
me to sign papers saying the captain was at fault. I
figured the captain was dead. What could it hurt?
Then Major Brown and Lieutenant Hardy, interrogation officers who normally questioned the enemy,
grilled me for twelve hours solid. They said the press
wanted to interview me. I had to answer their questions the way they wanted or else." He opened his
shaking hands toward Morgan. "Honest, Captain, I
didn't know you were still alive."

Morgan clenched his fists, feeling a fresh wall of
anger rise within him. He felt Laura's hand on his
shoulder, as if she'd sensed his grief and anger. Looking up, he saw tears in her eyes. She was sensitive in
ways that he was not. If it wasn't for her gentle nature, he'd probably have beaten the answers out of
Miles. But she had Miles eating out of her hand.
Managing a tight smile, Morgan nodded his praise to
her.

"So you went along with the charade because you
wanted a fix?" Laura asked.

Giving a nod, Lenny wiped the tears from his eyes.
"Yeah, I did. I'm sorry, Captain. But it was either roll
over on this, or detox. When I got stateside, the press
was houndin' me. After three months I was discharged. Then somebody tried to kill me. I took off,
realizing I was a liability to those officers." He
shrugged. "I didn't wanna die, so I disappeared...."

Morgan glared at Miles. He was a coward of the worst kind. Getting up, he walked around the room. Laura's face mirrored his anguish.

"The only way you'll be safe is if the real truth gets out, Miles. Until then you're living on borrowed time. Those goons who tried to kill you years ago are still around. You know too much. What I need is your testimony in order to clear my name completely. That's the only way you'll truly be safe." He halted in front of Miles, gripping the back of the chair with both hands. "I've lived underground for seven years, Miles. I haven't been able to see my family or have any kind of decent life for myself. If you feel as badly as you say, you'll help me. Will you?"

Laura saw Lenny begin to squirm. "We already have the evidence," she told him softly. "Please come back to Washington with us, Lenny. You can stay at a drug rehab house and get decent food and care. Morgan won't let anyone harm you."

"Well—" Lenny whispered.

"Please, Lenny," Laura begged. She held his wavering dark eyes. The man was scared to death. The question was, who was he more afraid of? Morgan, or Armstrong and Young's old threat? Holding her breath, Laura waited those agonizing seconds while he made up his mind.

"I ain't had a decent meal since…a long time ago," Lenny admitted. He glanced warily at Morgan, then at Laura. "I guess I'll come. I'm gettin' tired of living in cold basements with cardboard for a bed."

Laura didn't know whether to cry or leap for joy. She held both reactions deep within herself. Morgan moved over to the phone.

"We'll book tickets on the first flight out of here for Washington," he told her grimly.

Lenny's thin eyebrows rose and he craned his neck in Morgan's direction. "You mean, I get to fly?"

Laughing softly, Laura placed her hand on Lenny's pitifully thin shoulder. "Only first class for you, Lenny." Her mind raced with other items that would have to be attended to. On the plane she'd discuss them in detail with Morgan.

"The only attorney you want to represent you is William Wendell," Laura told Morgan in a low tone. Sweating and nervous, Lenny sat across the aisle on the commuter flight heading for Washington, D.C.

Morgan kept one eye on Miles and keyed his focus to Laura's comment. "I'm going to need a lawyer with the personality of a barracuda to fight the military justice system."

Laughing, Laura slid her hand into his. "Believe me, Bill is the best. He's argued and won cases at the Supreme Court level. Bill is about six-foot-five, with sandy-blond hair and blue eyes. He wears a mustache, too."

Morgan managed a grin, feeling the first real hope in seven years that his life might get turned around. "Then the guy can't be all bad."

"He's the best," she repeated fervently. "I'll call him as soon as we get home."

Gently Morgan raised her hand and kissed the back of it. He held her luminous blue gaze that sparkled with happiness. "No," he said huskily, "you're the best. And I like the way you refer to your house as our home."

A sweet fire blazed through Laura, and she ached to lean those few inches and kiss his so-serious mouth. "It feels right," Laura admitted.

Smoothing several strands of blond hair from her cheek, Morgan said, "When this thing gets past the planning stage and we have all our proof gathered, you and I are going to sit down and have a long talk."

Nodding, she rested her brow against his powerful shoulder. "About the future?"

"About us."

Warmth stole through Laura and she was content to wait. Morgan was being overly cautious about their relationship, but she understood why. He didn't want his dreams to be pulled out from under him as they had once before. His life, his focus, was centered on one day at a time, not future dreams. Squeezing his arm, Laura closed her eyes, suddenly very tired. So much awaited them. Bill Wendell would have to be brought to the house, and a deposition taken from Lenny and Morgan. That would start the wheels of justice turning. Hopefully, in Morgan's favor this time.

"What do you think, Bill?" Laura asked, looking across the kitchen table at the impeccably dressed attorney.

Wendell's sandy-colored eyebrows rose. He glanced at Lenny, who sat at his left arm, then Morgan, who sat at his right. In front of him was all the evidence amassed via the documents. "There's no doubt in my mind that there was a cover-up," he began.

"You'll take my case?" Morgan asked.

Wendell grinned. "I wouldn't miss this one for the world." Thrusting his hand out to Morgan, he said, "Will you retain me as your attorney?"

Gripping Wendell's hand, Morgan nodded. "You bet I will." He liked the tall attorney whose favorite hobby was playing basketball. There was a hunterlike look in his eyes that told Morgan the mild-mannered lawyer possessed the necessary skills to pursue his case to a successful end.

Clapping her hands in delight, Laura got up. She poured everyone another round of coffee. "What now, Bill?"

Leaning back in the chair, Wendell scowled thoughtfully. "There are a number of ways we could proceed. One is through the civil courts right off the bat."

"There are other ways, though," Morgan growled, watching pleasure dance in the attorney's eyes. "Aren't there?"

"You bet there are, Morgan."

"What do you advise?" Laura asked, coming over and standing behind Morgan, her hands resting on his shoulders.

"I think I'm going to make an appointment with Senator Robert Tyler. He's committee chairman for the defense budget committee. Bob and I go back a long way."

"He's pro-defense. What makes you think he'll believe this new proof about Hill 164?" Morgan demanded, worried that a pro-defense senator might want to push anything that could embarrass the military under the carpet to keep the money coming into the services.

"You've been gone for seven years," Bill said. "Bob Tyler is a watchdog of sorts over the military. He can swing for or against them."

"Tyler's a man with a lot of integrity and clout," Laura added, her eyes shining with hope.

"Precisely," Bill agreed. "I want your permission to take depositions from you and Lenny, plus the rest of the proof, to Bob."

Morgan saw the joy on Laura's face. He wanted to see that same joy when he made love to her for the first time. Gently putting aside that aching need, Morgan nodded to the attorney. "Take it all to him, Bill."

"Great." Wendell got up. "I'll send a limousine over to pick up you and Mr. Miles in about an hour. We'll take your depositions and get the ball rolling."

Laura withheld the urge to throw her arms about Morgan after Wendell had left. Lenny Miles sat at the table, still wolfing down the cookies she had set there for all of them earlier. If possible, he was even shakier than he'd been—little more than frayed nerves. Laura was afraid Miles might not be fit to give a deposition as he entered the detox phase of becoming drug-free. As soon as his deposition was completed,

Miles would be taken to the nearest rehab center for help and counseling. She followed Morgan into the living room so they could have a bit of privacy. Sasha trailed at their heels, panting happily because they were home.

"Things are falling into place," Morgan murmured, pulling her into his arms.

"I'm so happy."

"I know." He leaned over, claiming her smiling lips, cherishing their softness and eagerness.

The doorbell rang. Morgan raised his head, frowning. "What is this? Grand Central Station?"

Reluctantly Laura pulled from his arms to answer it. "From here on it, I think it will be." She opened the door and her heart slammed against her rib cage. "Jim..."

The marine captain stood grimly before her, his eyes hard. "May I come in, Laura?"

Cold fear washed over her. Jim Woodward had found what he was looking for; there was no doubt. She stepped aside. "Come in."

Jim hesitated. "Is he here?"

"Yes."

Compressing his mouth, the captain entered the house, briefcase clenched in his left hand. His gaze shot to the left.

Laura shut the door, feeling the electric tension between Jim and Morgan. Without thinking, she placed herself between the two men, who bristled like angry dogs. "We know what you've found, Jim," she began quietly, hoping to defuse the explosiveness.

Slowly Jim took off his cap, his eyes never leaving Morgan. "You've been harboring a fugitive, Laura. His real name is Morgan Trayhern. He's a traitor to this country."

"I'm no more a traitor than you are, Woodward," Morgan ground out. What would the captain do with the information? Had he already handed it over to someone else? Called the police? Morgan tried to read the officer's angry features.

"Really?" Jim bit out. His eyes blazed with anger and he turned it on Laura. "You of all people, harboring a bastard like this. I never expected this of you, Laura."

She opened her mouth to defend Morgan, but it was too late. Morgan moved like an attacking tiger, grabbing Jim by the lapels of his khaki uniform and slamming him up against the wall.

"Keep her out of this," Morgan snarled in Jim's face. "Just tell me what you've done with the information you've got on me."

Gasping, Jim dropped the briefcase as Morgan's powerful hands around the neck of his uniform shut off his air. "N-nothing...yet..."

With a curse Morgan released him, breathing hard. "You'd better sit down, Captain. There's some information you *don't* know that's just come to light. In less than an hour, I'm giving a deposition, and so is Lenny Miles, to clear my name and my family's honor."

Blankly the captain looked at Laura, who stood at Morgan's side. "Deposition? Lenny Miles? What are you talking about?"

Gripping the officer's arms, Morgan pulled him away from the wall. "Get in the kitchen and sit down, Woodward. You're going to hear the real facts concerning Hill 164. Now get moving. I don't have long to convince you that I'm not a traitor."

Laura sat quietly as Miles repeated the story to Jim. Morgan shoved the documents under his nose, and the marine officer inspected them closely. Within half an hour, Jim's demeanor had gone from hostility to disbelief. A dull red color crept into his cheeks as Morgan finished the explanation.

"Looks like I owe you both an apology," Jim said.

Laura sighed. "Don't apologize, Jim. Just keep all this under your hat until Morgan's attorney can contact the right people."

Jim looked at Morgan. "You know what this means, don't you?"

"Clearing my family's name."

"More than that. It means a full congressional investigation. They hung you seven years ago, and if they reopen this case, the press is going to have a field day."

The doorbell rang. It had to be the limo driver to take them to Wendell's office. Morgan got up. "Only this time, Young, Hadden and his cronies are going to be on the hot seat, not me. Miles, let's go."

Lenny nodded, grabbing one more cookie and stuffing it into the pocket of his slacks.

Laura continued to sit opposite Jim. She saw Morgan give her a wink, and she raised her hand in farewell. "Hurry home," she told him, a catch in her voice.

Morgan felt his heart smother with yearning. Laura looked drained. It had been one hell of a day, and it wasn't over yet. "I'll be home as soon as I can," he promised.

Jim gave her an odd look once Morgan and Lenny had left. He pushed the photos of Morgan toward her. "Here, you'd better keep these for now. I retrieved them from the photo files."

Grateful for his loyalty, Laura took them. "Thank you, Jim."

"That guy means something special to you?"

She smiled. "Yes, he does."

"You haven't known him long."

"That's true, but I love him, anyway. I guess I did from the first."

Jim gathered up the rest of the files and placed them in a neat stack in the center of the table. "Lucky bastard." He grinned over at her. "I hope he appreciates you."

"I think he does," Laura admitted softly.

Rising, Jim asked, "Is there anything else I can do for you?"

"Yes. Get that classified document Clay Cantrell located in Section B of the central files on Operation

Eagle, Hadden and Armstrong. We'll need it for Morgan's defense.''

''No sooner said than done,'' Jim promised. He picked up his hat and settled it on his head. ''You know I'm doing this for you.''

Jim had always had a crush on her, Laura realized. ''Do it for Morgan. He's a fellow marine and deserves your help.''

Nodding, Jim snapped his briefcase shut and took it in his left hand. ''You're right. The man's been framed and his entire life destroyed.''

Laura stood in the quiet living room after Jim had left. The house felt empty and cool without Morgan's presence. What would tomorrow bring?

Chapter Eleven

Laura went to bed at ten, after receiving a phone call from Morgan. The depositions were taking longer than expected because Bill Wendell wanted every memory, every item that might be important, put down for the record. And Lenny Miles was in worse shape with every passing hour. Exhausted, Laura had taken a bath and slipped into a delicate white cotton gown that brushed her feet.

Her head still spun with worries and anxieties. Would Lenny continue to cooperate? What if he froze and refused to go before a Senate investigative hearing? How would that affect Morgan's case? Sighing, Laura turned on her side, closing her eyes. She missed

Morgan more every hour. He'd promised to be home by midnight.

"Be quiet," Morgan told Sasha as he entered the foyer of the house. It was a few minutes past midnight.

Sasha whined, thrusting her cold nose into his outstretched hand. Absently Morgan patted the Saint Bernard and tiptoed into the living room. All but one light was out. Laura was in bed, he was sure.

The house was dark and quiet as he walked back toward the bedrooms. His bedroom was all the way down the hall from hers. He glanced at her door and saw that it was ajar. Normally she kept it shut.

"Go to bed, Sasha," he said, and the Saint disappeared into the kitchen to lie down on her blanket.

Morgan moved down the hallway toward Laura's room. He nudged the door open, the light filtering in behind him. Laura lay beneath the pink comforter, asleep. Standing uncertainly, he soaked in her peaceful features hungrily. Her thin cotton gown had a boat neck, emphasizing the clean lines of her beautiful throat and delicate collarbones. His head was pounding with pain from the arduous hours of giving a deposition, but something pushed him farther into her room.

Laura stirred, her groggy senses alerting her to someone's presence. Barely opening her eyes, she saw Morgan's shadowy form backlighted.

"Morgan?" Her voice was raspy with sleep.

He came over and sat down on the edge of her bed, placing his hand over her blanketed hip. "I'm sorry, I didn't mean to wake you." God, but she was beautiful when she was waking up. The comforter lay at her waist, revealing the contour of her small breasts beneath the gown.

Smiling sleepily, Laura turned onto her back, searching his shadowed features. "You look so tired. It must have been rough to talk about all those things again. Did everything go all right?"

Laura's sensitivity never ceased to amaze Morgan. He reached out to caress her cheek. It was soft, yet firm. "It went fine. Miles managed to complete his deposition before he went into detox. The rehab people have him now. He'll probably have a rough night of it," he answered gruffly, watching the light and dark outline the swell of her breasts.

"It was just as hard on you, though in a different way."

"I'll have to go through it again in front of a Senate hearing if Wendell gets his way. Every time it gets a little easier."

Her breasts tightened in anticipation as his gaze lingered on them. Laura felt an almost tangible hunger radiating from him, stirring all her feminine desires to bright life. His hand had come to rest on the side of her neck, stroking her flesh gently. Each touch sent feathery tremors of yearning through her. Sliding her hand up his arm, she managed a soft smile. "I'll be at your side, just as your family will be. You won't have to go through this alone."

Morgan traced the graceful curve of her neck with his scarred fingers, watching her lashes flutter closed and her lips part provocatively. He felt her hand tighten on his arm. The screaming need to love her sheared through him. But it wasn't time yet. He hadn't been cleared, and there was no guarantee that he would be. With his thumb, Morgan caressed her collarbone, absorbing her reaction to his touch.

Fighting his desires, fighting what he knew both of them wanted, needed, he said in a low voice, "Tell me of your dreams, Laura."

A little sigh escaped her lips. Slowly she opened her eyes, melting beneath his burning gray gaze. Morgan's hand rested warmly against her shoulder. "Dreams?" she whispered.

A slight smile pulled at his mouth. Laura was shaken. All he would have to do was lie down beside her and take her into his arms. Every nerve in his body begged him to do just that, and quell the fire raging within him. "Yeah, dreams. Your dreams. What do you want out of life?"

It was nearly impossible to think coherently with Morgan continuing to stroke her neck and shoulder. There was such incredible gentleness in his eyes now, and in his voice. "When I was being shuttled from one foster home to another, I dreamed of having a family adopt me," she began in a wispy voice. "And after Mom and Dad did adopt me, I dreamed of making them proud of me."

"And so you graduated with honors from Georgetown University," Morgan said, his voice thick, unsteady.

She ran her fingers up the length of his corded forearm, feeling the muscles tense beneath her caress. "Yes. And then, one by one, they died. Since then, my dreams have changed."

"How?" Morgan lifted his hand, smoothing away the wrinkles on her brow, then began to thread his fingers through her blond hair, which glinted with highlights as he moved the strands.

Her scalp tingled with pleasure as he sifted the hair through his fingers. Laura swallowed convulsively and inhaled sharply, unable to speak.

Laura's answer was far more important than his own selfish desires, and Morgan stopped coaxing his fingers through her hair. Her blue eyes were huge and luminous, telling him of her need of him. "What kind of dreams do you weave in your sleep now?" Morgan coaxed her huskily.

Breathless beneath his tender onslaught, Laura struggled to contain her yearning. It would be so easy to sit up and slide her arms around his shoulders, drawing him down into bed with her. But their coming together had to be a mutual decision, and she gently acquiesced to that realization.

"Children mean so much to me," she began softly. "My dreams aren't very exciting, Morgan. I hoped to one day find a man I could love. Who would want children as much as I do."

"You'd make a hell of a mother," Morgan told her, still caressing her hair. Forcing himself to stop touching her, he placed his hand at his side. Disappointment was mirrored in her eyes, and he felt like a first-class heel.

Laura lay in the ebbing silence, absorbing Morgan's introspection. "What are your dreams?"

"I won't have any until this hearing is over." Morgan saw the despair come to her eyes. He wanted to tell Laura that he saw her as his wife and the mother of his children. But it was far too soon to say any of those things. They'd barely known each other a month. Everything was moving too swiftly. And yet, as he studied her in the dim light, the soft curves of her face highlighted, Morgan knew that a month was time enough. "When it's over," he whispered, "I want to share my dreams with you."

"That time won't come soon enough," Laura murmured.

Rising slowly to his feet, Morgan gripped her hand. "I know ... Get some sleep, little swan. I'll see you in the morning."

Morning. Laura watched Morgan slowly retreat from her bedroom. As the door was quietly shut, darkness once again descended around her. The love she felt for Morgan was close to exploding. It was so hard not to tell him how she felt. But he'd had so much taken from him already, she knew that he didn't want to risk anything in the future, for fear the present would once again undermine him. Tears stung Laura's eyes, and she blinked them away. The future...their future, hung in precarious balance. Burying her face in the goose down pillow, she wondered how Senator Tyler would react to the evidence Bill Wendell would present to him.

"Senator Tyler wants to see all of us," Wendell told Morgan over the phone late the next afternoon. "I sent the depositions over to his staff this morning, and I just got a call from him."

Grimly Morgan asked, "What's his mood? Does he believe me?"

"The senator, at this point, is incredulous. He wants you, Miles and Laura at his office in an hour. Can you make it?"

Checking his watch, Morgan muttered, "Yes, we'll be there."

"Excellent. I'll have one of the rehab staffers bring Miles over. I guess he's in pretty rough shape this morning. I'll meet you there, Morgan. Goodbye."

Placing the receiver back on its cradle, Morgan glanced up at Laura. She looked like a young girl in her pale-pink cotton dress with lace at the collar. Its pearl buttons gave the dress a decidedly old-fashioned air. She was his Laura, the idealistic dreamer, and she was beautiful in his eyes.

"The senator wants to see us," he said.

Her eyes widened. "He does?"

"All three of us. He's read the depositions, and I think he wants to see if we're real or a figment of Wendell's imagination."

Laura's heart started beating hard. Grabbing her lavender raincoat to face the typically showery April day, she tried to smile. "I'm ready."

Laura waited impatiently in the foyer for Morgan to get his dark-brown corduroy sport coat. He reappeared and shrugged it over his shoulders, offering her a tense smile. *Please,* she prayed, *let the senator believe Morgan.*

Bill Wendell met them outside the senator's office, briefcase in hand. He smiled at them. "Come on, don't look so glum," he chided. "This isn't an inquisition."

Morgan kept his hand cupped over Laura's elbow. "I wish I shared your optimism, Bill."

Wendell slapped him on the back. "Relax. All the senator wants to do is ask you some questions. Miles is already here—a little worse for wear, but he's coherent." He opened the door and stepped in after Laura and Morgan.

Morgan took in the walnut-paneled outer office. Mementos from Senator Tyler's long and illustrious career filled the walls. His secretary, Alice, was dressed in a gray business suit and gave them a welcoming smile. Miles sat quietly on a chair.

"Hello, Bill," Alice said. "Go right on in. The senator's waiting." She stared at Morgan.

Laura felt him tense beneath the secretary's piercing gaze. Was it curiosity or a look damning Morgan as a traitor? She wasn't sure. Following the men, she entered the sumptuous inner office last.

Morgan saw a white-haired man in a pin-striped suit stand up from behind the huge cherry-wood desk. Tyler was short, reminding Morgan of a bull. His eyes were a piercing dark brown, his jaw set, with sharp creases on either side of his thin mouth. If he didn't know better, Morgan would have mistaken him for a military commander.

Tyler came around the desk and walked energetically over to them. He halted in front of the group, his eyes snapping to Morgan. "You're Captain Trayhern."

Morgan nodded, slowly taking the man's parchmentlike hand. Tyler had to be close to seventy. "Ex-captain, sir."

"Quite right. Thanks for coming." Brusquely Tyler motioned to leather wing chairs that had been placed in front of his desk. "All of you, sit down."

The room crackled with energy. Morgan sat on the edge of his chair, his hands clasped between his legs; he was expecting the worst. Tyler's shrewd gaze never left him, and he had the feeling that the senator was sizing him up.

"I've got to tell you, Bill, you sure as hell threw a bomb into my office with this information." Tyler jabbed a short, square finger at the depositions.

Wendell smiled slightly. "Bomb or not, Senator, I think Morgan Trayhern deserves a hearing based upon the evidence."

Tyler's straight white eyebrows drew together. He addressed Morgan. "Who else was in that room with you when General Armstrong was dying?"

"Armstrong's doctor and the maid."

"So there were witnesses."

"Yes, sir."

"Young isn't going to willingly testify that Armstrong or he told you anything. You know that?"

"If I were in Young's shoes, I'd roll over and play dead, too," Morgan began slowly. "He's got everything to lose."

Tyler exploded with a bark of laughter. "Son, you've got a string of generals and CIA people who will fall like dominoes if we go into hearings on this. You can bet your last bottom dollar they're going to protect one another's backsides right up the line."

"Just like they did after Hill 164," Morgan ground out.

"I'm afraid so." Tyler leaned back in his chair, surveying him for long, tension-filled moments. "I know your father, Chase, very well. And I'm well aware of your family's prestigious history in defending our country. Every son and daughter of your family has served with distinction. I'll tell you, if Bill had said it was anyone but a Trayhern, I wouldn't have touched this case with a ten-foot pole."

Morgan's heart thumped hard. He swallowed, his eyes widening on the senator. "Then you'll help us?"

Tyler got up and moved around his office. "Earlier today, Captain Jim Woodward came here. He brought me irrefutable proof there has been a cover-up. I'm not at liberty to share those documents with you because they're top secret. Only Committee members for the hearing can read them."

Morgan turned in the chair, watching the senator closely. "Can you give us an idea of what they say?"

Returning to his chair and sitting down, Tyler grinned. "Basically, they tie together all the threads of your documents. Hadden, who is now a CIA assistant chief, was at the bottom of all this. It was his idea to pin the rap for Hill 164 on you. My guess is that Armstrong wanted his general's star more than he wanted to take the heat for the tactical error he and the CIA had made. You know Armstrong was up for promotion at the time of Hill 164?"

"No, sir, I didn't," Morgan rasped.

"And Young, who was already a general, had his tail in a sling because he'd approved your company's move to Hill 164. The documentation ties the three of them together, that's all I can say."

Laura leaned back. Jim Woodward had turned out to be Morgan's friend, not foe. She could hardly wait to throw her arms around the marine captain and thank him for his thorough work on Morgan's behalf.

"So," Tyler went on, "I'm calling a secret investigative committee hearing tomorrow morning."

"Wait a minute," Morgan said, rising. "Why secret? If I'm going to be exonerated of these charges, I want it public, Senator."

"Morgan—" Wendell protested.

"No!" Eyes blazing, Morgan looked at both men. "You don't understand. My family has gone through hell. My father was forced to retire. My brother Noah's career with the Coast Guard has been jeopardized. People treat him like a leper, and he's had to bust his butt to get assignments that should have come a hell of a lot easier." His breathing became hard with feeling. "And my sister, Alyssa, has been castigated at the Naval Academy *and* Pensacola. She was given the silent treatment all those years." Morgan braced his hands on the senator's desk and stared at him. "Do you have any idea what that's like? Frankly, I don't see how Aly stood it. How would you like to be ignored for four years, Senator? No friends. No one to talk to. No one to study with." He straightened, anguish in his tone. "This hearing goes public or not at all, Senator. If you won't agree to that, then I'll have Mr. Wendell pursue my case through civil court proceedings. It might take longer, but I intend to vindicate myself and my family publicly. Anything less than that isn't acceptable."

Tyler slumped back in his leather chair and eyed Morgan. "You've got your father's fighting spirit, you know that?"

"I don't have a choice in this matter," Morgan grated. "My family's honor is at stake. My *life* is at stake. And to be honest, Senator, I'm fed up with running and hiding."

Laura bowed her head, fighting back the tears that flooded her eyes at Morgan's pain.

"There are senators and congressmen who will shred you if you go public, Trayhern."

With a sharp laugh, Morgan straightened. "What the hell can they possibly do to me that hasn't already been done?"

"Your family will be put through more public scrutiny," he warned. "Do you want Noah and Alyssa to take more pressure from their peers?"

Morgan snarled, "If they've made it this far, they'll hang tough the rest of the way. Our family was bred to win, Senator, not lose. We don't give up."

Rubbing his pronounced chin, Tyler muttered, "That's obvious." He stared down at his desk for well over a minute, then said finally, "You realize that if the inquiry were in secret, General Young and Hadden would be more apt to come clean. In a public hearing, they're going to hire the best criminal defense lawyers they can to appear before the television cameras."

"America believes I'm a traitor," Morgan said fervently, "and they believe my family is little better than that. If I can't clear my name in front of the public, no one in my family, including me, will ever have a decent life. It's bad enough my life has been screwed up. But to see my brother and sister, not to mention *their* children continue to carry this burden, is asking too much."

Tyler shot Wendell a grizzled look. "He's right, you know."

Wendell nodded. "Will you contact someone over at the Justice Department? Warrants will have to be served on Young and Hadden."

"I'll make that call as soon as you leave." Tyler looked over at Lenny. "Mr. Miles, you will be given protective custody by my committee. They'll make sure you have a place to stay during this hearing. Does that meet your requirements?''

Lenny nodded, unable to meet the senator's piercing gaze. His brow was beaded with sweat, and he squirmed uncomfortably in the wing chair. "Uh...yes, sir.''

Laura stood. "Wait a minute," she pleaded. Everyone quieted and looked at her. "I'm sorry for barging in, but I have a question, Bill."

"Well...sure. What is it?''

Nervously Laura said, "If Morgan were to have a wire placed on him and he went back to Young and Hadden to force them to admit their part in the coverup, could that possibly cut short a long hearing? I mean—'' she licked her lower lip, glancing at the senator ''—if Morgan got their admission, how could they refute it in a public hearing?''

"Young lady, you're right," Tyler agreed with a grin. "That's something neither of us thought of, Bill."

Wendell nodded.

Hope shone in Laura's eyes as Morgan went to her side. He gave her a tender smile. "You're something else," he told her.

"I'll call the Justice Department and talk to them about that possibility. Morgan, would you be prepared to try it?''

He turned, slipping his arm around Laura's waist. "Yes, sir.''

"It might be dangerous," Tyler warned. "If Young and Hadden can throw your life away to protect theirs, to say nothing of the threats made to Mr. Miles, they might resort to more physical means of getting rid of you this time.''

Gravely Morgan nodded. ''It's a risk I'm willing to take.''

''Fine. I'll have someone from the Justice Department contact you shortly. Planning will have to be done on how we can lure Young and Hadden into meeting you.'' He waved his hand at them, already picking up the phone. ''Nothing we've talked about leaves this room, understood?''

Everyone nodded.

Outside, after Lenny had left with Bill, Morgan drew Laura to a halt.

''That was a good idea,'' he congratulated her.

''I'm not so sure now,'' Laura said, frowning. ''What if Young or Hadden think that killing you is the best way to solve the problem?''

''That,'' he whispered, leaning over to kiss her wrinkled brow, ''isn't going to happen. Come on, let's go home. I don't know about you, but I'm hungry.''

Laura poked at the food on her plate, unable to eat. Things were moving too quickly to suit her. She had barely gotten the meal on the table when Ken Phillips from the Justice Department had called. He would be coming over shortly to discuss Morgan's meeting with Young and Hadden.

''You okay?'' Morgan asked, looking across the table at Laura.

''Yes and no.''

"I never realized what a worrywart you are, Laura Bennett," he teased gently.

Rallying beneath his cajoling, Laura forced a slight smile. She put her fork aside, her stomach tied in knots. "I guess I'm not cut out for all this cloak-and-dagger stuff."

He reached out, catching her hand and giving it a squeeze. "But here's the lady who gave us the idea."

She met his deep gray gaze, needing to be held by him but knowing that was impossible right now. "If this will force Young and Hadden's hand, then it's worth it, Morgan."

The doorbell rang. "That must be Phillips," Morgan said. Releasing Laura's cool, damp fingers, he rose and went to answer the door.

Laura cleared the dishes away so that Ken Phillips and Morgan could sit and plan. She liked Phillips immediately. He was in his mid-thirties, with military-short black hair and intelligent hazel eyes. And it was apparent that Morgan liked him, too. Both men were basically military types who appreciated cutting through red tape and getting to the heart of a matter.

"We've placed a tap on Young's and Hadden's residential and office phones," Phillips told him. "Tomorrow morning you're going to call Young and demand a meeting. Tell him you're getting tired of your Legion job and want another assignment. When you meet Hadden and him in person, try to get them both to admit to their parts in the affair."

Morgan nodded, studying the wire he'd wear tomorrow morning. "And you'll have your men in a truck, taping the conversation?"

"Yes. We'll also be providing you protection. If things start going bad, use the code word 'Brazil'. We'll come on the run."

Laura shivered as she placed the plates in the sink. Why wasn't either man particularly upset over the possibility that Young or Hadden could pull a gun?

Phillips grinned. "I don't think they'll wait long to have a meeting with you once that call is placed."

Morgan shook Phillips's thin but strong hand. "Thanks."

"I'll be here at eight in the morning. You'll make the call to Young's office at nine. By then I'll have the wire on you, so you can go directly to the meeting, if necessary."

"Sounds good," Morgan said. He rose and walked Phillips to the door. Ambling back into the kitchen, he saw how upset Laura had become.

"How you doing, little swan?" he asked, bringing her into his arms.

Closing her eyes, Laura slipped her arms around his waist, resting her head against his shoulder. "Okay."

"It will be over soon, sweetheart. I promise."

She stirred at the endearment. "I don't want to lose you, Morgan. Not after all this," she whispered, fighting back tears.

"Shh, you aren't going to lose me." He chuckled and held her tightly, rocking her gently back and forth. "I'm too mean to die. And look at me. I've got everything to live for."

Battling to gather her strewn emotions, Laura choked out, "Just be careful, Morgan."

He released her enough to place a finger beneath her chin. Her blue eyes, once sparkling with hope, were dark with despair. The urge to kiss that trembling lower lip tore him apart. "I'll be very careful," he promised her huskily. If he didn't let Laura go, he was going to carry her into her bedroom and love her. How many times, just before a battle, had he wished to be in a woman's arms, safe and loved?

"Come on, it's almost midnight. Let's turn in. We've got a big day ahead of us tomorrow."

It hurt to move away from Morgan. Swallowing her pain, Laura mutely agreed and left the kitchen to go take her bath. Tonight she wanted to be with Morgan, no matter what he thought or wanted. She shut the door to the bathroom and leaned tiredly against it. Her world as she knew it had suddenly grown bleak. The possibility of losing Morgan to a bullet tore a sob from her. Covering her mouth with her hand, she sat down at the vanity, trying to cry quietly so that Morgan would never hear her.

Chapter Twelve

Morgan had just turned out the light in his bedroom and was getting ready to remove his terry-cloth robe, when there was a knock on the door. He opened it. Laura stood uncertainly before him, dressed in her floor-length cotton gown.

Laura's throat constricted as she raised her gaze to meet his turbulent gray one. Placing a hand against her breast where her heart beat wildly, she whispered, "Don't send me away, Morgan...."

The hesitation, the longing, were all Morgan heard in her low, unsteady voice. Her fragility broke his ironclad grip on himself, and he offered his hand to her. "Come here," he said thickly.

Stepping forward, Laura reached out, sliding her hand across his cheek where the scar lay in silent testimony to the pain he'd borne alone for so many years. She heard the swift intake of his breath. "Tonight," she murmured, "is for both of us. I don't know what will happen tomorrow. I'm afraid, Morgan...."

With a groan, he swept Laura into his arms, violently aware of the softness of her breasts, of her willowy length sinking against him. "I am, too," he admitted, cradling her face, looking deeply into her lustrous blue eyes.

"Love me?"

He ran his mouth lightly across Laura's parted lips. "Yes," he rasped. "You're so sweet and kind, my little swan." He gathered Laura into his arms, carrying her to his bed. The moon provided just enough light to see her features as he set her gently on the bed. Sitting next to her, he watched as she raised her hands.

Her fingers trembling, Laura unknotted the belt at his waist, then pushed the robe away from his shoulders. His chest was broad and deep, tapering to a flat, hard stomach. Her breath caught, and her eyes filled with anguish. "Oh, Morgan..." and she stared at the terrible scars that ran vertically down each side of his heavily muscled chest. "I didn't realize," she cried, touching them, feeling the puckered flesh beneath her fingertips.

He tunneled his fingers through her damp hair, inhaling her sweet scent. "It's all right," he said thickly, trailing a line of kisses from her temple, across her cheek, to seek and then find her lips. Lifting her chin, Morgan imprisoned Laura's face within his hands. "Don't cry." He kissed away the silvery tears that had beaded on her lashes.

"How much you've suffered." Laura wept, kissing him hungrily, wanting to absorb his pain and loss—to replace them with joy. Their joy.

Laura was lush as he plundered her mouth, and he heard her moan with pleasure. Just the gentle touch of her hands against his chest took away all his memories. Laura was his present, his future. Her breath came rapidly, sweeping across his face as he devoured yielding lips that drove him beyond every wall he'd ever hidden behind.

Breathing hard, too, Morgan ran his hands across her slim shoulders, pushing aside the straps to her gown, pulling the fabric downward. Her flesh was so soft, yet firm, as she was. He watched her flushed face fill with delight as he cupped her small breasts in his hands. Each was a proud crescent, curved and firming under his. As he grazed each expectant nipple, a little cry broke from her and she swayed in his arms.

"Beautiful," he groaned, pressing her back against the bed. She was so small and yet so exquisite as he undressed her. In the moonlight, her skin was translucent ivory, her eyes dark with invitation as he skimmed his hand from her hip back up to her awaiting breasts.

The instant Morgan's mouth captured the first nipple, Laura cried out, pressing herself against his naked body. His flesh was taut, the muscles powerful against her yielding form. His callused fingers incited blazing fires wherever he touched her. Her world dissolved beneath his knowing, exploring hands. The tight knot of need deep within her grew, the moist heat building between her thighs, telling him of her need for him.

"Easy, my little swan," Morgan coaxed thickly, bringing her beneath him. She was fire and water, hot and liquid, as he parted her curved thighs. The pleading look in her eyes grew as he slid his hand beneath her hip. He was shaking with need. She was so small, but so incredibly fiery, burning through all his control. The sheen to her flesh emphasized her beauty as he brought her to him.

Morgan's name was on Laura's lips as he thrust deeply into her. A little cry of pleasure, of triumph, slid from her exposed throat. She moved her hips upward, bringing him deep within her, wanting nothing more. Morgan's body moved slickly against hers and she gripped his shoulders, calling out his name as the heat built, then erupted within her. Sunlight burst within her as she closed her eyes, feeling his lean, powerful thrust. A softened smile pulled at her lips as she felt Morgan stiffen, then grip her hard against him. In that rainbow moment, Laura cried out with him, glorying in their untrammeled union, their love indelibly stamped on each other.

A rivulet of sweat traveled down Morgan's left temple. Laura leaned upward, kissing it away. She fell back into his arms, smiling weakly. "I love you," she whispered.

The words, softened heartbeats to his ears, made him want to hold Laura forever. He smiled down into her shining blue eyes, which were filled with love for him alone. "How long have you known?" Morgan asked huskily, running several damp strands of her hair through his fingers.

Laughing weakly, Laura murmured, "Forever, I think...."

He moved his hips slightly, seeing the desire rekindle in her eyes. She was so small and tight, yet able to accommodate him. Hadn't she been able to deal with him in all ways and all levels from the beginning? "I used to dream about the woman who would one day be my wife," he told her, kissing her temple, then her cheek, his mouth finally coming to rest against her smiling lips. "She would have the courage to hold me when I was weak. And she would have the fire to stand on her own without me." He nibbled at her lower lip, running his tongue across the yielding texture of it. "And most of all, she would love me and love the children I'd want to share with her."

Tears gathered in Laura's eyes as she held his tender gaze. Despite the terrible atrocities committed against him, Morgan was able to unveil and share his gentle inner core with her. Sliding her hands up across his cheeks, she whispered, "You're my dream come true, darling. I don't think I fit all the requirements of your dream, though...."

He chuckled, kissing each of her fingers in turn. "Nonsense. Inside that little frame of yours is a backbone of pure steel." Morgan drew her index finger into his mouth, biting it gently, watching the flame of need grow brighter still in her lustrous blue eyes. "And fire—" He groaned, releasing her fingers, "Little swan, you've got all the fire a man could ask for." Sweeping his hand down across her damp form, he angled her hips upward. "I see the fire right now...."

A moan tore from Laura as she felt his returning power filling her once again with throbbing life. She closed her eyes, bringing him into pulsing rhythm with herself. Each thrust, each groan from him, drove her to new, dizzying heights. His mouth ravished her lips, setting her free, coaxing her to become wanton within his arms. It was so easy giving her heart, her soul, to Morgan. The sunlight burst once more within her, and she fused with him, accepting his love, his need of her as they climbed and reached that pinnacle of beauty simultaneously.

Morgan fell against Laura, his head next to hers. They were both breathing hard, their flesh slick and heated against each other. He rolled off her, then brought her on top of him. Her lips were swollen from the demands of his kisses, but they were beautifully pouted as she smiled down at him. He moved his fingers through her golden hair, glorying in the wonderful smile in her eyes. "You're the woman I want to carry my children, Laura."

The words, filled with raw emotion, made Laura's heart contract with happiness. She closed her eyes, reveling in his fingers as they gently massaged her scalp. "I will," she promised huskily. As she moved her hands across his chest, she once again felt the ridges of those scars. Leaning down, she kissed the length of each one, wanting to take away the memories of years filled only with agony and loneliness.

Morgan lay back beneath her ministrations, feeling the feathery touch of her lips against his chest. He closed his eyes, his hands moving slowly up and down her back, tracing the indentation of her slight but strong spine. Just Laura's worship of his body had begun to erase so many ugly memories that had haunted him. Her fingers were trembling as she lightly stroked the scars on his chest. He forced his eyes open to slits, watching her innocent features bathed in moonlight and shadow. "How can you take pain away?" he asked hoarsely.

Laura smiled wistfully and reached up, sliding her fingers down the scar on his face. "Love takes pain away, darling. It always has."

Her voice was tremulous, a breeze wafting across a summery, flower-filled meadow. Laura was part goddess, part sweet innocent, part fiery woman. Gathering her in his arms, Morgan guided her to his side. Raising up one elbow, he studied her rapturous features in the moonlight. "I love you," he whispered, cradling her cheek, holding her simmering gaze. "And when this is all over, I want the time we deserve together.'' He brushed a droplet of perspiration from her unmarred brow. "We haven't had any since we met, Laura. Neither of us. We've been on a collision course with life."

"Tell me about it," she said with a laugh, sliding her hands around his neck. His face was completely devoid of tension now, and she realized how boyish he looked in that poignant moment. Sobering, she held his molten gaze. "After this is over, we've got all the time the world has to offer us, Morgan."

Lazily he smiled. "Don't get that worried look in your eyes, sweetheart. Everything's going to be fine tomorrow."

Would it? Laura bit back the words. "One day at a time," she murmured, pushing him down on his back and leaning across him. "Tonight, all I want to do is love you," she said breathlessly.

Her silky hair spilled across his face and he inhaled her special feminine scent as he reached up and kissed her cheek. "Come here, my flighty little swan," he growled, holding her against him, pulling up the sheet. As he closed his eyes and Laura fitted against him, he knew he held his new life, his new world, in his arms.

Morgan awoke slowly. He felt the exploring touch of Laura's hand against his chest, trailing down his torso. With a groan he forced open his eyes. It was dawn, and she looked beautiful sitting there, the sheet gathered around her waist. He saw the concern in her eyes. As her hand moved back up across his chest, he brought her into his arms, kissing her slowly, tasting the depths of her mouth.

"I'm dreaming," he said, his voice rough with sleep.

Laughing softly, Laura shook her head, then rested her brow against his. "No, you're not. I'm sorry I woke you, but I couldn't resist touching you. You've got such a beautiful male body, Morgan Trayhern."

He grinned, running his hands down her spine, cupping her hips. "Adore me all you want, sweetheart."

She smiled and kissed his strong mouth. "Conceited, brazen animal."

The scent of her entered his nostrils, and Morgan nuzzled his face into the strands of her blond hair. "You turn me into an animal, little swan," he growled. "It's all your fault."

Laura struggled out of his arms and knelt beside him, her hand resting against his chest. She could feel the sledgehammer beat of his heart beneath her palm. "Morgan, I want you to know that no matter what the outcome of all this, I'll be with you."

Her sudden seriousness jolted him. Stroking her arm with his fingers, he said, "You've stuck with me through all this."

"No," she said, "you don't understand." She chewed on her lower lip, searching for the right words. "No matter what happens, Morgan—whether you prove your innocence or not—I'm going with you. If that means leaving America, then I'll do it."

The tears in her eyes wrenched at his heart. Sitting up, Morgan put his arms around her. "You'd go back to France with me?"

Laura nodded.

Sighing, Morgan held her for a long time. "When did you decide this?"

"Weeks ago," Laura admitted, her voice choked with tears. "You mean more to me than any country, Morgan. After we made such beautiful love last night, I don't think I could ever bear to be away from you again."

"My sweet woman," Morgan murmured, kissing her gently. Wiping the tears from her cheeks, he gave her a game smile. "You've run the gauntlet with me, haven't you? And you'd run it again, if you had to." He saw the vulnerability in her stormy blue eyes, but her inherent strength was also there. "In a few hours, if we're lucky, this whole thing will be over, and we can plan our life here, in America."

Laura stood in the gloomy light of the police van, listening to the last-minute instructions being given to Morgan by Kevin Phillips. The phone call Morgan had placed to General Young's residence had netted instant results. It was nearly noon, and that was when Morgan was to meet Young and Hadden at the general's country home.

How could they look so calm, when she felt as if her stomach were tearing apart? Phillips wasn't happy about the fact that their van was stationed three miles from the manor. But if they got any closer, Young might spot it and become suspicious. The operation could be compromised, and Morgan's life placed in jeopardy as a result. Morgan would drive to the manor in a rented car. Laura gnawed on her lip, her eyes never leaving him. He wore a white shirt, a tan corduroy blazer and dark-brown slacks. His face was set and hard. There was a gleam in his gray eyes that sent a shiver of dread through her.

Laura leaned against one of the steel counters, near a policeman, who sat at the console with a set of earphones on his head. Tape machinery, radio gear and video equipment were crowded into every nook and cranny of the van. There was hardly any room to maneuver, except up and down a narrow aisle. Morgan would drive up the long quarter-of-a-mile asphalt road to the manor. He'd have no weapon on him except for a deadly looking military knife, strapped to the inner calf of his right leg and hidden by the trouser.

Phillips glanced at the watch on his wrist. "It's time for you to leave. We'll follow at a safe distance."

Morgan nodded his thanks to the agent and moved to where Laura stood. He saw the absolute terror in her eyes. Giving her a smile meant to defuse her worry, he took her into his arms. She came, warming the coldness he carried deep within him. Kissing her hair as she buried her face against his shoulder, Morgan whispered, "Everything's going to be all right, Laura."

Tears gathered unexpectedly in Laura's eyes. She blinked them away. Morgan didn't need her weeping right now; he needed her strength. Standing on tiptoe, she kissed him longingly. His mouth was hot as it claimed hers with an urgency that ripped the breath from her.

Tearing his mouth away, Morgan looked deeply into her gray eyes. "I love you," he rasped. "Never forget that...."

And he was gone. Laura sat down, her knees wobbly in the aftermath of Morgan's claiming kiss. Phillips came over and sat down next to her as the van started up, ready to follow Morgan's car at a safe distance.

"He's going to be fine, Laura."

"I hope so."

Phillips smiled. "Morgan's a soldier first, and he's as tough and smart as they come. I don't think many men can outfox him when the chips are down."

The praise for Morgan's abilities left her cold. "If he's going up against men carrying weapons, he doesn't have a chance."

"You're forgetting one thing."

Laura chewed on her lower lip. "What?"

"He's a Trayhern. That says it all."

After parking the car next to a Mercedes-Benz and a BMW, Morgan got out. The manor where Young lived was an impressive three-story brick home with white columns in front, testament to its Southern heritage. Thirty-foot-high rhododendrons blossomed in pink and white profusion around the residence, creating a protective green wall.

The cries of birds filled the wooded area surrounding the manor, as Morgan sauntered up the brick walk. His senses were screamingly alert, and his nostrils flared to catch any unusual or foreign scents. In the large picture window he saw a tall, spare man with black horn-rimmed glasses watching him intently. That was Richard Hadden. Earlier Phillips had shown him pictures of the CIA agent. There was a dangerousness to Hadden. He had the face of a weasel with those dark, deeply set eyes, gleaming with a fanatical light.

Before Morgan could knock, General Paul Young pulled open the door. His jowly face was set, his hazel eyes narrowed and assessing.

"Come in, Trayhern," he growled.

Morgan entered the spacious, highly polished foyer. Everything about the house bespoke understated wealth. Young was dressed in a gray cardigan, a white shirt and black slacks. His mouth was compressed.

"In there," the general ordered gruffly, pointing toward the living room.

The hair on Morgan's neck stood on end as he walked into the room filled with antiques and green plants. Hadden waited tensely, his hands knotted. Hatred flowed through Morgan as he studied the thin agent. He swung his attention to Young, who stood by the picture window after closing the drapes.

"Now what's this all about?" Young demanded.

"Not so fast," Hadden growled, advancing toward Morgan. "Let's search him. I don't trust—"

Morgan gripped Hadden's hand as he extended it toward him. "And I don't trust you, Hadden," he snarled softly, holding the man's glare. If the agent discovered the wire, the operation was doomed. Morgan tightened his fingers around Hadden's wrist and pushed him away.

Rubbing his arm, Hadden backed off. "How do we know you aren't armed?"

"How do I know you aren't?" Morgan shot back. There could be a pistol in a holster beneath the agent's green wool sport coat.

"Richard, relax," Young snapped. He turned his attention to Morgan. "Now what do you want?"

"I've got my full memory back, General."

Young's brows furrowed. "So?"

"So I know that you and Armstrong lied to me about being a CIA mole in the Legion. I'm not really a mole, am I?"

The general reached into a humidor, then jammed tobacco into a pipe. "Nonsense. The CIA has a file on you. Legally you're working for them."

Morgan maneuvered around so that his back was to a wall and he could see both entrances to the living room while keeping an eye on the two men. "I want a new assignment. Living in the Legion isn't exactly rewarding."

"Money?" Hadden muttered. "Is that what this is about? You want us to pay you to keep your mouth shut?"

"What do I have to spill, Hadden?"

"Plenty!" the agent shot back, going over to a wing chair and sitting down. "Unfortunately, before Armstrong died he admitted he set you up."

"You set me up, Hadden."

"So what if I did? It was in the best interests of this country."

Anger serrated Morgan. He put a clamp on it. "I have to hand it to you," he told the agent. "That was a pretty creative answer for the way Armstrong and Young screwed up on sending my company to Hill 164."

Rolling his eyes, Hadden muttered, "Look, Trayhern, a lot of good officers' careers were at stake."

"It was more than that," Young growled. "Don't forget, Richard, it was *your* decision and plan we reluctantly agreed to in sending Trayhern's company in there in the first place."

The agent waved his hand airily. "I wasn't the only one who made mistakes on gathered intelligence data, Paul."

"No, but your faulty decision making cost my men's lives," Morgan whispered, wanting to advance across the room and beat the living hell out of the smug agent.

"Look, Trayhern, it wasn't my fault you lived. Word came back that you'd survived with brain damage." A catlike smile crossed his mouth. "The two tough military geniuses were panicking. Armstrong and Young were ready to throw in the towel, until I came up with the idea of altering your past. And it was pure brilliance on my part to place you on assignment in the French Foreign Legion. You were out of sight, out of mind, and the American public accepted you as the scapegoat."

Morgan held on to his disintegrating self-control. "What about Lenny Miles?" he ground out.

Hadden shrugged. "He was a junkie. I couldn't pin the rap on him. He was too unstable. So I had the interrogation officers scare the hell out of him and make him sign a confession that you were at fault." He scowled. "The hophead disappeared stateside three months after we discharged him. He's probably dead in some back alley by now."

"Quick, clean and simple," Morgan said, hatred vibrating in his voice.

The general lit his pipe and puffed hard on it. "Look, we're sorry it had to be you. But that's the past, Trayhern. What is it you want now? A new billet? More money? Tell us, and we'll get this settled. I can't afford to have you loitering around in the U.S. Someone might recognize you."

Hadden got to his feet, his hand moving inside his sport coat in one smooth action. "Don't move, Trayhern," he snarled as he held out a Walther P-38 pistol with a silencer on it.

"Richard! What the hell are you doing?" Young exploded.

The agent grinned. "Hands up, Trayhern. I'm sure Miles is long dead. Now it's time to get rid of the last survivor of Hill 164. You and I are going for a long walk behind the general's house."

Slowly Morgan raised his hands. His heart thudded hard in his chest. He watched Hadden advance on him, a lethal look in his squinted eyes. "You kill me, and you've got murder on your hands," he whispered.

Young cursed. "Don't do this, Richard! Dammit, I don't want any more blood spilled!"

"Shut up, Paul. You've always been the squeamish one about Operation Eagle." He waved the pistol to the right. "Down that hall, Trayhern. Keep those hands above your head. Any dumb moves, and I'll shoot. Move!"

"Tell me something," Morgan snarled, "you ever been to Brazil?" He knew the code word for help would bring Phillips and his people on the run. But would it be soon enough?

Startled by the question, Hadden laughed. "Pal, I'm not interested in discussing travel plans with you. Get moving!"

How long before Phillips and his people could arrive? Morgan slowly turned, in no hurry to leave the house. Even if they did get here in time, that was no guarantee they could save his neck. As he walked down the shadowy hall toward the rear door, his mind swung sharply to Laura. My God, she had heard this conversation—she was in the van with Phillips and his team. All her fears had come true.

"Open the door," Hadden growled. "And hurry up!"

Sunlight poured through the trees bordering the well-kept backyard. The beauty of the daffodils, tulips and hyacinths contrasted starkly with the terror Morgan felt. The lawn sloped toward a dirt path that went through a heavily wooded area. Hadden jabbed the barrel of the Walther into his back as they headed toward it.

"Get moving or I'll blow your head off right here!"

Increasing his pace, Morgan entered the woods. By the time Phillips arrived, it would be too late.

"Why are you doing this?" Morgan asked.

"I don't want any loose ends. I've got my pension coming in two years. I'm not jeopardizing my neck for yours. No one will know the real story behind Hill 164. You'll die the traitor the public thinks you are, Trayhern."

Hatred twined with anger, and the word *traitor* grated across Morgan. In one swift motion he turned, lifting his right leg and aiming the toe of his shoe at the pistol Hadden held. He saw the agent's eyes widen, but it was too late. The tip of his shoe met Hadden's arm. The Walther discharged, the shot muted by the silencer.

"Sonofabitch!" Hadden screamed as the pistol flew high into the air. He lurched after it.

Morgan tripped Hadden, throwing himself on top of him. They landed hard on the path. Hadden struck upward, the punch connecting solidly with Morgan's jaw. He tasted the salt of blood in his mouth. Parrying a second blow, he doubled his fist and smashed it into Hadden's sneering face. Pain soared up his wrist and into his arm. There was a sharp crack. Hadden screamed, blood flowing heavily from his broken nose.

Breathing hard, Morgan threw the agent onto his belly and pinned one arm behind his back. The Walther lay only a few feet away from them, to the left of the path. Hitching up Hadden's arm until he screamed in pain, Morgan eased off the agent, using his foot to bring the pistol within reach. Gripping it, he loosened his hold on Hadden's arm.

"Get up," Morgan rasped, straightening and backing away. "Hands behind your head, Hadden."

The agent crawled slowly to his knees. Glaring at Morgan, he staggered to his feet, doing as he was instructed.

Morgan wiped the blood from his lip and chin, and jerked his thumb in the direction of the manor. "Let's go back. The Justice Department is waiting for you." He grinned, even though it hurt like hell.

"Wh-what are you talking about?" Hadden stumbled up the path, weaving unsteadily.

"Our entire conversation was taped, Hadden. I'm wearing a wire." Elation soared through Morgan at the agent's gasp of disbelief. They made their way out of the woods and climbed up the expanse of lawn.

Just as Morgan stepped onto the patio, he saw Phillips and two of his men, dressed in flak jackets and armed with M-16 rifles, come bursting through the rear door. Relief showed on Phillips's face as he gestured to the men to halt.

"You okay?" he asked Morgan, surveying Hadden grimly.

"Yeah, just a split lip and some loose teeth." Morgan pushed the agent toward the men with the rifles. "Take him into custody." Glancing at Phillips, he said, "I think we got enough on tape to throw the book at them."

Grinning, Phillips gave orders to have Hadden handcuffed and read his Miranda rights. "You did a damn fine job, Morgan. With this evidence I believe the senator will be able to make a public press statement about your innocence."

"No hearings?"

"Doubtful. Even if Young and Hadden refused to admit to their part in Hill 164, this conversation will incriminate them. Come on, I've got one anxious lady waiting for you in the van. We wouldn't let Laura come in with us under the circumstances. She's about ready to throw a shoe."

Morgan nodded, taking a handkerchief from his back pocket and holding it to his lips. "I'll bet she is." Hesitating at the door, he turned to Phillips. "Do me a favor?"

"Sure."

"Give me a little time to calm the lady."

Smiling, Phillips slapped him on the shoulder. "You got it."

Laura stood by the van, her hands gripped in a tight knot of fear. She'd heard over the taping system that Morgan was alive. When she saw him appear out the front door, she flew down the brick walk.

Morgan halted, opening his arms to her. With a muffled cry, Laura threw her arms around his neck. Laughing softly, he embraced her tightly.

"I'm okay, little swan," he murmured, inhaling her delicious scent.

Laura's breath came in huge gulps. "I was so frightened—"

"Shh, so was I, sweetheart. Everything's fine. Believe me." And Morgan gently pushed her away just enough so that she could see he was all right. Tears shimmered in her blue eyes, and he leaned down to kiss them away.

"You're hurt."

"Just scratches."

Shakily she touched his injured lip. Blood had splattered across his sport coat and shirt. "I was so afraid, Morgan."

"I know," he said, caressing her mussed hair. He gave her a slight smile. "It's over now."

Swallowing her fear, Laura nodded. "Does Phillips think there's enough information to clear your name without a hearing?"

Morgan nodded. "Plenty. The senator will probably call a press conference as soon as he can, and I'll be vindicated." Laura looked clean and untouched after the violence that had surrounded him minutes earlier. Cupping her chin, Morgan smiled down into her eyes, now lustrous with love for him alone. "What do you say we go home, call my folks and then plan the rest of our lives together?"

Laura smiled through the tears and slid her hands upward, brushing the cheek with the scar. "I'd like that."

"I love the hell out of you, Laura." Morgan put his arm around her shoulders, and they walked back to the van. The singing of the birds took on added meaning for him, and so did the bright April sunlight. It was spring, the time of year for new seedlings to sprout, for flowers to poke their heads above the wintry, barren ground and blossom. New beginnings, he mused. He gazed tenderly at Laura, who returned his look with love.

There was so much he was grateful for because of her presence, her loyalty and her undying belief in him. Leaning down, Morgan kissed her temple. "You know what? I'm going to enjoy spending the rest of my life telling and showing you just how much I love you."

Sinking against him, Laura closed her eyes, the terror receding, to be replaced by hope. She felt his strength, his protection, where she was concerned. Meeting his warming gaze, she whispered, "Let's go home. We've run the last of this gauntlet together. The first day of our life is about to begin.''

Morgan nodded, leading her past a bright patch of red tulips toward the rented car in the distance. ''Home,'' he murmured, a catch in his voice, ''sounds good.''

* * * * *

The LOVE AND GLORY series continues with the spine-tingling, heart-touching story of how the Trayhern parents, Rachel and Chase, first met and loved—coming soon from Special Edition!

Silhouette Intimate Moments®

AWARD OF EXCELLENCE

NORA ROBERTS
brings you the first
Award of Excellence title
Gabriel's Angel
coming in August from
Silhouette Intimate Moments

They were on a collision course with love....

Laura Malone was alone, scared—and pregnant. She was running for the sake of her child. Gabriel Bradley had his own problems. He had neither the need nor the inclination to get involved in someone else's.

But Laura was like no other woman . . . and she needed him. Soon Gabe was willing to risk all for the heaven of her arms.

The Award of Excellence is given to one specially selected title per month. Look for the second Award of Excellence title, coming out in September from Silhouette Romance—**SUTTON'S WAY**
by Diana Palmer

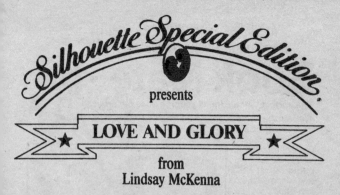

Silhouette Special Edition

presents

LOVE AND GLORY

★ ★

from
Lindsay McKenna

Introducing a gripping new series celebrating our men—and
women—in uniform. Meet the Trayherns, a military family as proud
and colorful as the American flag, a family fighting the shadow of
dishonor, a family determined to triumph—with
LOVE AND GLORY!

June: **A QUESTION OF HONOR** (SE #529) leads the fast-paced
excitement. When Coast Guard officer Noah Trayhern offers
Kit Anderson a safe house, he unwittingly endangers his own
guarded emotions.

July: **NO SURRENDER** (SE #535) Navy pilot Alyssa Trayhern's
assignment with arrogant jet jockey Clay Cantrell threatens her
career—and her heart—with a crash landing!

August: **RETURN OF A HERO** (SE #541) Strike up the band to
welcome home a man whose top-secret reappearance will make
headline news . . . with a delicate, daring woman by his side.

You'll flip . . . your pages won't!
Read paperbacks *hands-free* with

Book Mate · I

The perfect "mate" for all your romance paperbacks

**Traveling • Vacationing • At Work • In Bed • Studying
• Cooking • Eating**

Perfect size for all standard paperbacks, this wonderful invention makes reading a pure pleasure! Ingenious design holds paperback books OPEN and FLAT so even wind can't ruffle pages—leaves your hands free to do other things. Reinforced, wipe-clean vinyl-covered holder flexes to let you turn pages without undoing the strap . . . supports paperbacks so well, they have the strength of hardcovers!

Pages turn WITHOUT opening the strap

SEE-THROUGH STRAP

Reinforced back stays flat

Built in bookmark

BOOK MARK

BACK COVER HOLDING STRIP

10 x 7¼ opened
Snaps closed for easy carrying too

Silhouette Intimate Moments®

COMING IN OCTOBER!
A FRESH LOOK FOR
Silhouette Intimate Moments!

Silhouette Intimate Moments has always brought you the perfect combination of love and excitement, and now they're about to get a new cover design that's just as exciting as the stories inside.

Over the years we've brought you stories that combined romance with something a little bit different, like adventure or suspense. We've brought you longtime favorite authors like Nora Roberts and Linda Howard. We've brought you exciting new talents like Patricia Gardner Evans and Marilyn Pappano. Now let us bring you a new cover design guaranteed to catch your eye just as our heroes and heroines catch your heart.

Look for it in October—
Only from Silhouette Intimate Moments!

Silhouette Romance

LONG, TALL TEXANS

Diana Palmer brings you the second Award of Excellence title

SUTTON'S WAY

In Diana Palmer's bestselling Long, Tall Texans trilogy, you had a mesmerizing glimpse of Quinn Sutton—a mean, lean Wyoming wildcat of a man, with a disposition to match.

Now, in September, Quinn's back with a story of his own. Set in the Wyoming wilderness, he learns a few things about women from snowbound beauty Amanda Callaway—and a lot more about love.

He's a Texan at heart . . . who soon has a Wyoming wedding in mind!

The Award of Excellence is given to one specially selected title per month. Spend September discovering *Sutton's Way* #670 . . . only in Silhouette Romance.

RS670-1R